THOROUGHBRED

DATE DUE

FEB 0 9 2010	
JUL 3 0 2012	
ILL 5-23-16	
ILL 10-6-2016	
MAY 1 0 2022	

GAYLORD   PRINTED IN U.S.A.

HarperEntertainment
A Division of HarperCollins*Publishers*

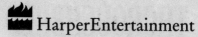

HarperEntertainment

A Division of HarperCollins*Publishers*
10 East 53rd Street, New York, NY 10022-5299

This is a work of fiction. The characters, incidents, and dialogues are products
of the author's imagination and are not to be construed as real. Any
resemblance to actual events or persons, living or dead, is entirely coincidental.

Produced by 17th Street Productions, a division
of Daniel Weiss Associates, Inc.

HarperCollins books are available at special quantity discounts
for bulk purchases for sales promotions, premiums, or fund-raising.
For information please write:
Special Markets Department, HarperCollins Publishers, Inc.,
10 East 53rd Street, New York, NY 10022-5299.

ISBN 0-06-106542-0

HarperCollins®, ®, and HarperEntertainment™ are trademarks
of HarperCollins Publishers, Inc.

Cover art © 1998 by Daniel Weiss Associates, Inc.

First printing: December 1998

Printed in the United States of America

Visit HarperEntertainment on the World Wide Web at
http://www.harpercollins.com

❖ 10 9 8 7 6 5 4 3 2 1

Why couldn't I just keep my mouth shut?

"She's the property of the humane society, and I'm the head of its fund-raising committee. I'd like to have a better look at her."

"Sorry," Ashleigh said. "She was really upset when you all crowded around before, and I think she's had enough for one day."

"I can't see how bringing her out of her stall is going to upset her," the woman cut in. "I'm sure the owner of the farm would agree. And anyway, aren't you awfully young to be working as a groom? Can we speak to your manager?"

Ashleigh bristled. "I'm the owner's daughter," she said through gritted teeth. "I'm the one who found Lightning. I brought her food and helped rescue her. I've taken care of her almost all by myself because my parents knew I'd do a good job. I really care about her—a lot. The humane society hasn't done anything except come here and look at her once in a while." As soon as the words were out of her mouth, Ashleigh regretted them. She knew she'd made these people angry, and that would do nothing to encourage them to let the Griffens adopt Lightning. *Oh, no. I blew it,* she thought. *Why couldn't I just keep my mouth shut?*

A HORSE FOR CHRISTMAS

"I can't believe the transformation!"

Dr. Frankel, Edgardale Farm's regular vet, stepped away from the white mare he'd just examined. He turned to ten-year-old Ashleigh Griffen, who was anxiously gazing over the stall door in the big horse barn, and smiled. "Lightning looks great," he said.

Ashleigh glanced at her parents, who were standing beside her, and grinned happily. She'd been hoping that's what the vet would say. Her parents smiled back approvingly.

Dr. Frankel continued. "The physical improvement in this horse since I first examined her is incredible. I never thought she'd recover so quickly considering the state she was in. I'd say she's gained between 400 and 500 much-needed pounds. She's bright, alert. I didn't think you could do it, young lady," he said to Ashleigh, "but you have. You've definitely proven me wrong."

Proving the vet wrong had been exactly what Ashleigh had intended when she'd heard Dr. Frankel's pessimistic outlook for Lightning five months ago. Ashleigh was so pleased. She stroked Lightning's white, velvety nose.

"And I bet you loved every minute of it," the vet added with a twinkle in his eyes.

Ashleigh nodded. "I sure did." Caring for Lightning hadn't been hard—it had been fun—but she understood why the vet had originally had doubts. Lightning had been a terrible mess when she first arrived at Edgardale. She was all skin and bones, shaggy-coated, and filthy. There were bloody welts on her back where her former owner had whipped her. It was awful to see a horse in such sad shape.

Ashleigh and her best friend, Mona Gardener, had first discovered the mare that spring when they'd stumbled upon a rundown farm and found a horse tied up in a filthy stall. The horse was thin, weak, and dull-eyed. She'd been left with neither food or clean water and stood with her head hanging low.

The girls returned to the farm a few days later, bringing feed and hay to the mare. They began to call her Lightning, for her brilliant white coat. One day Ashleigh found the mare's owner viciously beating Lightning. She rode home to Edgardale Farm in tears of despair to ask her parents for help. Ashleigh's father had immediately called the humane society, but before anyone could act, Kurt Bradley, the Griffens' stable manager, brought the mare to Edgardale. He'd taken matters in his own hands, notified the police about what he was about to do, and had gone up to the farm to get Lightning.

After humane society officials assessed the mare's condition, the police had charged her owner with animal cruelty, and the humane society welcomed the Griffens' offer to stable Lightning at Edgardale until decisions were made about the mare's future. They had a standard six-month waiting period in abuse cases with large animals, since they needed to be sure the animal was completely healthy before considering final adoption. The local weekly newspaper had picked up Lightning's story and ran it on the front page with heart-wrenching pictures of the mare the day after her rescue. But Lightning had made giant strides since then. Thanks to Kurt and Ashleigh's hard work, she was now a beautiful, fit horse.

"I can see that you've been conditioning her, too," Dr. Frankel said, breaking into Ashleigh's reverie.

Ashleigh nodded. "I started by walking her on the paddock lanes—just to get her muscles going. When she put on some weight and seemed stronger, Kurt helped me longe her. Now I can work her by myself, although Kurt usually still helps."

"Good strategy. The mare has definitely benefited from it. Have you found out any more about her background?"

"No," Mr. Griffen answered. "All the former owner said to the police was that he had bought her cheap at an auction and didn't know anything about her history. By the way, he's in jail now. It turns out he was wanted on several other crimes, too."

Dr. Frankel nodded gravely. "That's exactly where he belongs if he could abuse an animal as badly as he abused this mare. Although I do have to forewarn you, Ashleigh, that when horses have been abused like this, they sometimes do strange and unexpected things. Keep that in mind when you're working with her. Be careful."

"I will," Ashleigh said solemnly, although she couldn't imagine Lightning behaving badly or meanly.

"Well, let me have a look at your weanlings," Dr. Frankel said to the Griffens as he left the stall.

As her parents and Dr. Frankel headed down the barn aisle, Ashleigh hurried into Lightning's stall and hugged the mare, who greeted her with an affectionate nicker. "You're so great, Lightning. I love you so much," Ashleigh said softly.

Lightning stood just over fifteen hands at the withers and her white coat gleamed. Ashleigh admired her silky, white mane and tail, and the muscle that covered the ribs, shoulders, and hips that once protruded from her body. In the past five months, a brightness had come into Lightning's once-dull eyes, and Lightning had grown as attached to Ashleigh as she was to the mare. Ashleigh so desperately wanted to keep her for her very own. But in the end, it would be up to the humane society to decide.

Ashleigh took Lightning's halter off its hook outside the stall and buckled it over the mare's head. Mona was coming over after school and together they would work Lightning in one of the paddocks.

No one at Edgardale knew exactly how much training Lightning had had in the past, except that her former owner had worked her in harness, so she'd been accustomed to bridle and bit. Since Dr. Frankel estimated Lightning to be between ten and twelve years old, there was a good possibility that she had been trained under saddle, too. Lightning was gentle and mild-mannered, but because she'd been so badly abused before coming to Edgardale, they were taking her retraining and conditioning slowly, letting her adjust to her new surroundings and circumstances gradually.

Ashleigh looked up to see Mona coming down the barn aisle. The two girls were similar in height and build—both slim and athletic—but Ashleigh's brown hair was straight and shoulder-length, while Mona's was short and curly. "Hi, you guys. So what did the vet say?" Mona asked.

Ashleigh smiled to her friend. "He couldn't believe how good she looks."

"That's what I thought he'd say," Mona replied as Ashleigh led Lightning out of her stall.

"You know, Ash, every time I see her, I just can't believe how different she looks—how much better. She's really starting to look so beautiful. I wonder if she has some Thoroughbred blood in her."

"Dr. Frankel said she might," Ashleigh said. "But she can't be a purebred. He said she's a little heavier-boned than most Thoroughbreds, and she's got a dished nose, so she might have some Arabian in her, too. But I don't care what her breeding is. I think she's perfect."

Ashleigh rubbed her cheek against the mare's head before clipping the longe line to her halter and leading her out of the barn. Brilliantly colored autumn leaves drifted down from the trees like snowflakes, covering the ground.

"It would be so neat if you could keep her," Mona said. "Then we would both be getting horses for Christmas."

Ashleigh shot her friend a surprised look. "Your parents said they're definitely getting you a horse as a Christmas present?" Ashleigh asked.

"Not exactly, but they keep hinting around. I'm pretty sure they wouldn't do that if they'd definitely decided not to. Anyway, have your parents heard anything from the humane society yet?" Mona asked.

Ashleigh shook her head. "Not yet. I guess we won't hear until the six-month waiting period is over."

"And it almost is," Mona said. "It would just be so amazing if you could adopt her! The humane society would be crazy not to let you. Your farm is a perfect home for her."

"I know," Ashleigh agreed. "I can just imagine the two of us galloping up the lanes, racing each other. I'll pretend I'm a jockey riding in the Kentucky Derby."

"And I'll pretend I've made the Olympic equestrian team," Mona added.

"And someday we'll both get what we want," Ashleigh said. "You'll have big horse farm and lots of jumpers, and I'll be racing Thoroughbreds!"

"Well, it's something to dream about," said Mona with a grin.

"My father always says that if you don't have big dreams, you'll never get what you really want."

"He's probably right. Guess I'll have to start dreaming more about my horse farm. Let's see, how many stalls do I want? Maybe an indoor ring..." Mona mused.

Giggling, the girls planned out Mona's imaginary farm, which, of course, would be next door to Ashleigh's racing stable. By the time they'd reached the paddock, Mona's farm had become a real palace, and one of Ashleigh's horses had won the Kentucky Derby.

Ashleigh began circling Lightning at a trot on the end of the longe line. Like the hub in the center of a wheel, Ashleigh turned with the mare and watched her movements. She thought Lightning was moving really well, but she wasn't really experienced enough to be sure.

Then she noticed that another spectator had joined Mona at the paddock fence. It was Kurt. Kurt was in his thirties but he already had gray hair. Ashleigh knew there was a reason for that. He'd lost his only child—his ten-year-old daughter—a year ago when she'd died of leukemia. Kurt had told Ashleigh all about it when he'd helped to rescue Lightning. He had always been very quiet and withdrawn, but Ashleigh's parents said helping her with Lightning seemed to have given Kurt a new lease on life.

"Good, good," Kurt called to Ashleigh. "See how

she's got her head down? Her neck's arched, and she's working forward."

Ashleigh nodded, pleased with herself and Lightning. She'd been right in guessing Lightning was moving well. She couldn't wait for the day when she would sit on the mare's back and *feel* her smooth strides.

"Bring her down to a walk," Kurt called. "Change direction and try the trot again."

A half hour later they finished their session. Ashleigh gave Lightning some well-deserved treats before putting her back in her stall and brushing her.

After Mona had set off on her bike for the short ride home, Ashleigh walked out to the paddocks where the farm's ten broodmares were grazing. In paddocks nearby were the mares' weanling foals. They had grown tremendously over the summer and in early September, they had been weaned from their dams. Farther on, the larger yearlings were grazing. Two colts in Edgardale's crop of yearlings had already been sold privately. The others would be sold at the big fall auction in a week's time where the Griffens hoped they would bring top prices. After having cared for the yearlings from birth—almost two years—

Ashleigh would be sad to see them go, but selling the yearlings was how her parents made their money and what kept Edgardale thriving.

It is such a beautiful place, Ashleigh thought. She couldn't imagine living anywhere else. Tree-lined paddocks stretched into the distance over rolling hills and the white fences separating them gleamed with fresh paint. Best of all were the magnificent Thoroughbreds contentedly grazing on the lush grass.

Ashleigh watched as Wanderer—a big, black mare with striking conformation and an imposing air—nudged Jolita—a chestnut with a lovely white blaze—away from a tasty patch of clover she was coveting for herself. Just beyond them, Zip Away was rolling in the grass and turning her coat into a dirt-streaked, grass-stained mess. Each horse had a very distinct personality, that was for sure.

The horses were all special, but Wanderer was Edgardale's prize broodmare. She'd had a successful race record before her retirement, and her foals all showed great promise. One of her offspring, Wanderer's Quest, a three-year-old filly who'd been born at Edgardale, was racing that year in stakes company, and Ashleigh's parents were eagerly following her career. The whole family had been at Churchill Downs on Kentucky Derby Day to watch the filly come in a close second in the Aegon Providian Mile. During the summer, she'd raced in several other graded stakes races, two of which she'd won, and another in which she'd come second. If she continued putting in winning performances, she would become the most successful horse ever bred at Edgardale. Quest's racing accomplishments also raised the value of her dam, Wanderer. Any of Wanderer's new offspring would surely bring more money to the Griffens at auction. In fact, Quest was running in a major race that weekend at Belmont, in New York, and Ashleigh intended to glue herself to the TV to watch.

When Ashleigh entered the kitchen of the family's modest farmhouse to do her homework, her older sister, Caroline, was sitting at the kitchen table, polishing her nails. Caroline was two years older than Ashleigh, and the sisters couldn't have been more different in their looks and interests. Caroline was blond and blue-eyed, like their mother. Ashleigh had inherited her father's brown hair and hazel eyes.

Their five-year-old brother, Rory, came bounding into the room. "Ash, you're taking me riding on Moe after dinner, remember?"

"Umm . . ." Ashleigh replied. She hadn't remembered.

"But you promised!" Rory cried.

"All right," Ashleigh said, "but we're going to stay in one of the paddocks."

Rory pouted. "How come?"

"Because you don't listen to me when we're on the trails—you're always trying to race ahead on Moe. Until I can ride Lightning and keep up with you, you have to ride in the paddocks."

"I'm not a baby!" Rory protested, shaking his blond mop of hair. He, too, had inherited his mother's looks.

"Talk to Mom and Dad," Ashleigh said. "They're the ones who made the rules."

"All right, but I want to canter him," Rory insisted.

"Okay, but only on the longe line," Ashleigh responded, then chuckled as Rory stomped out of the room.

"I don't know why you're laughing, " Caroline said, waving her hand to dry the polish. "You were just as stubborn at his age, always wanting to do more than you were allowed."

Ashleigh frowned thoughtfully. "Yeah, I guess I was." She selected an apple from the fruit bowl on the table and shined it on her shirt, then grabbed the latest issue of the *Daily Racing Form* off the counter.

"Not that it's any of my business, but I hope you're

not going to spend the rest of the afternoon reading that," Caroline said, glancing at Ashleigh, "instead of doing your homework."

"I'm doing my homework first!" Ashleigh shot back. Since Lightning had come into her life, she'd been working extra hard to keep her grades up. Now, instead of getting lost in a horse magazine and then rushing through her homework, she got her homework done first. Ashleigh didn't want to give her parents *any* reason to change their minds about adopting Lightning. And if she brought home a bad report card, she knew they would have one.

Caroline laughed. "Listen to you! Homework first? Boy, you must really want to keep that horse."

Ashleigh made a face at her sister, then turned and hurried upstairs to their bedroom. Caroline didn't realize that her remark had hit home. Ashleigh really did want to keep Lightning—more than anything.

Saturday afternoon, Ashleigh had the television set tuned to the pre-race coverage of the Belmont Grade 1, mile and a quarter race for three-year-old fillies— the race that Wanderer's Quest would run in. It was an important race for fillies, and if Quest won it—or was even in the top three finishers—it would be a notch in her belt and could set her on the road to the Breeder's Cup races in late fall.

When the camera focused on Quest in the saddling paddock, Ashleigh was instantly reminded of the precocious foal Quest had been three years before. Ashleigh remembered their romps around the paddock, with the little filly almost always outsmarting her. She'd had a feeling then that Quest would be something special.

Quest certainly was gorgeous—tall for a filly and built like her mother, Wanderer. Her black coat gleamed like coal in the sunlight as she eyed the crowd surrounding the Belmont saddling paddock, prancing and arching her neck. *She's showing off,* Ashleigh thought, smiling. Then she looked around, wondering where her parents had gone. They wouldn't want to miss this.

She could hear their voices in the kitchen, and two unfamiliar female voices, too. *Maybe someone has come by to look at the yearlings,* Ashleigh thought. Then she heard one of the unfamiliar voices say, "The humane society has been considering . . ." Ashleigh couldn't hear the rest of the sentence, but her heart was suddenly in her throat. *The humane society?* she considered excitedly. *Are they here to talk about Lightning? Maybe they'll tell my parents I can keep her!*

2

There was a long commercial break before the race began, and Ashleigh jumped up from her cross-legged position on the rug and went to the living room door. She could hear more clearly from there.

"The mare is very happy here," Ashleigh heard her mother say. "You've seen her—she looks wonderful, a different horse altogether."

"Yes. A remarkable improvement."

"We were hoping our daughter could keep Lightning. We would love to adopt her . . ."

The voices were so quiet that Ashleigh had a hard time hearing everything, but her mother's words made her tremble with excitement.

"We understand," another unfamiliar voice said, "and this would be a lovely home for the horse, but the society . . ."

Ashleigh wanted to dash into the kitchen and beg

them to let her keep Lightning, but she knew that would only make them stop talking.

"The society appreciates what you've done . . . a remarkable improvement. . . . Your generosity . . . exceptional. . . . We'll be in touch. . . ."

The voices faded.

Ashleigh rushed back to watch the race, but her thoughts were clouded with worry. The women hadn't sounded like they were ready to go through with the adoption. In fact, it sounded like they were stalling. *What will happen to Lightning?* Ashleigh wondered. *Will she be allowed to stay at Edgardale?*

Quest was making her way to the gate as Ashleigh rushed to a window looking out over the drive. She saw two women wearing the type of tweed skirts and sweaters she had always associated with the rich people who came to the sales rings at Keeneland. The women walked to their elegant, gray car and drove off. Ashleigh felt confused. From the little bit she had overheard, she wasn't sure what was going to happen. She had to find out from her parents what they'd been discussing in the kitchen. But for now, she had a race to watch.

Ashleigh hurried back to the TV just as the race was about to go off. She put her thoughts about that conversation momentarily to the side as she watched

Quest—black and elegant just like her mother—load into gate number five.

Despite Quest's previous record, the bettors didn't seem to have any confidence in her. She was going out at odds of fifteen to one. Long odds for a horse with Quest's racing history. *Have the bettors seen something in Quest's current condition that I missed, or are they just betting their personal favorites?* Ashleigh thought that must be the case, since a New York–bred horse had the most favorable odds. Ashleigh's parents always tried to bet on the horses they'd raised. Ashleigh hoped they'd bet on Quest today.

Three more fillies loaded after her. Then there were the tense minutes waiting for the gates to open. Finally, they were off! Ashleigh focused her eyes on Quest's saddle cloth. She was number five.

Ashleigh's parents hurried into the living room and sat down on the couch as the gates opened. The track announcer began his call. Ashleigh kept her eyes on Quest. She would talk to her parents about Lightning once the race had been run.

"Gateway takes the lead, followed by Brightangle, then Goer's Lady. As expected, Wanderer's Quest is just behind the leaders." The announcer rattled off more names and positions, but Ashleigh wasn't listening. Her eyes were glued to Quest as the filly stayed in mid-pack down the backstretch and into the far turn.

Ashleigh's stomach was in knots as she willed the filly to start moving up through the pack, but she wasn't sure the horse could. Quest was competing against the classiest company she'd ever faced. Goer's Lady and Gateway were both multiple Grade 1—the highest stakes level—winners. Quest had never won better than a Grade 3 race.

Ashleigh heard her parents urging the filly on, too.

"Gateway still has the lead by a length and a half as the field sweeps around the far turn," the announcer called. "Behind her, it's Goer's Lady and Brightangle fighting it out. The top three have six lengths on the rest of the field. It looks like the favorite today, Gateway, is going to go gate to wire."

Ashleigh banged her fists on the carpet in frustration when the television camera cut to the first three runners in close-up and ignored the rest of the field. She didn't know where Quest was or what she was doing. Her mind crept back to thoughts of Lightning. Ashleigh couldn't wait to ask her parents what the women from the humane society had said. *Have they made a decision?*

At the top of the stretch the camera angle suddenly widened and the announcer cried, "Wanderer's Quest coming up on the outside!"

Now Ashleigh saw Quest racing up quickly outside of the leaders. The filly was eating up the track, coming on like a freight train.

"Wanderer's Quest is coming up on Goer's Lady's flank," the announcer's call continued. "Now she's sweeping by Brightangle, forging ahead to challenge Gateway."

"Go!" Ashleigh and her parents screamed at the television screen. "Come on, girl!"

None of them breathed as she got closer and closer to winning, with only a few yards to go to the wire.

The two horses swept under it. It was so close. *Had Quest's nose been in front, or Gateway's?* Ashleigh wasn't sure. Neither was the announcer, whose call was, "Too close to call!"

The PHOTO sign flashed on the infield board. Ashleigh glanced at her parents, who shook their heads in uncertainty over the finish. Ashleigh felt tense as she waited for the final results to be put up. She knew from what her parents had taught her, and from all the reading she'd done, that the racing stewards would study the photo taken at the finish and determine from it which horse had won. Once in a while there was a true dead heat where both horse's noses went under the wire at exactly the same time, but that was rare.

Ashleigh heard her father mutter, "Boy, I hope she got it. What do you think, Elaine?"

"It looks like she might have gotten the head bob," Mrs. Griffen answered, "but it was really hard to tell."

Ashleigh kept her eyes keen on the track. Quest's and Gateway's jockeys were still out on the track, circling their mounts in front of the grandstands until the winning horse's number was posted on the infield board. The other horses in the race were being led back to the stabling area.

The infield board flashed. The letters lit up, OFFICIAL RESULTS. A second later Quest's number came up in first place. Her odds, since she'd gone off at fifteen to one, would pay huge dividends.

Ashleigh's parents had placed a modest bet on Quest before the race, but they had won big time. They jumped up off the couch with shouts of joy. "One of our foals just won a Grade 1!" Ashleigh's father said. "I can hardly believe it!"

"Neither can I!" Mrs. Griffen cried. "This is such good news for the farm."

The television showed the winner's circle presentations. Ashleigh saw the Fontaines, Quest's owners, looking pretty excited in the winner's circle, as Wanderer's Quest was led in.

I'm going to be there someday, Ashleigh thought. *I'm*

going to be riding one of those winning racehorses and standing in the winner's circle.

Then she turned to her parents, "What did the humane society people say?" Even in the excitement of the race, Lightning had never been far from her mind.

"That they were happy with Lightning's improvement," Mrs. Griffen answered.

"Did they say we could keep her?" Ashleigh asked.

"For the time being, yes, but they haven't made any decisions yet." Her mother frowned.

"But why?" Ashleigh exclaimed. "This is a perfect home for Lightning!"

"Well, the six-month waiting period isn't over yet," Mr. Griffen explained. "They need to run a lot of checks and monitor the horse's condition before they can go through with the adoption process. They have to make sure she's fit. . . ."

"But *we're* the ones who are *getting* her fit!" Ashleigh cried.

"I know," her father said, shaking his head. "I think it's silly, too, that at this late stage they won't make a decision. It's what your mother and I would call bureaucratic red tape. Anyway, we told them again that we were very committed to adopting Lightning. They certainly can't complain about the excellent care she's had since she's been with us." He put his hand on Ashleigh's shoulder.

"We're very proud of the work you've done with Lightning, Ashleigh," her mother said. "You're doing a great job and you haven't let your homework or chores slip either."

Ashleigh had worked hard with Lightning, and it was true that her grades hadn't slipped. But she was still worried. "I love Lightning so much. I just don't know what I'd do if I couldn't keep her," she sighed.

Both her parents smiled. "Well, let's take this race as a good luck sign," Ashleigh's father said with a chuckle. "Okay, let's get out to the barn and get the horses settled. We're already behind schedule since we stopped to watch the race."

Ashleigh was distracted as she did her evening chores. She couldn't stop thinking about her parents' conversation with the women from the humane society. *Why hadn't they made a decision about Lightning's adoption? She had a perfect home now.* She wondered if there was something the humane society wasn't telling her parents.

Ashleigh, Caroline, and Rory helped Kurt give the horses their evening feeds and fresh water after bringing them in from the paddocks. Then they went up to the house for dinner, while Kurt headed up to his own apartment over the barn office and tack room.

Mrs. Griffen had put dinner in the oven before they'd gone out to tend to the horses. The kitchen was filled with mouthwatering aromas. Everyone pitched in with the household chores as well as the barn chores. Ashleigh quickly set the table, since it was Caroline's turn to do dishes. Rory was still too young to be put in charge of either task, since he couldn't reach the cupboards or the sink.

Over dinner, the Griffens discussed the week ahead. The remaining yearlings would soon be going to auction at Keeneland and it was time to get them ready. The yearlings had to be in top condition and relatively well-mannered when they went into the sales ring. All of the yearlings had already been broken to halter and lead line, but some of them could be high-spirited, and needed to practice walking quietly at the end of the lead. The Griffens couldn't afford to have them misbehave on the auction podium. Well-mannered yearlings generally brought better prices.

"Ashleigh," Mr. Griffen asked, "if you have some extra time tomorrow, maybe you could work with a couple of the yearlings on the lead line, walking them around one of the paddocks?"

Ashleigh had planned to spend the next day working with Lightning, but she could see that her father's face reflected his usual pre-auction worry. In many ways, it was the biggest day of the year for them—the day when they earned money for their efforts over the previous year. Ashleigh knew it was important to help out before the auction.

"Sure, Dad," Ashleigh said, her thoughts still on Lightning. "I'll work with them."

"Can I help?" Rory asked, giving his parents a pleading look.

Mrs. Griffen considered. "Hmmm . . . I guess, if you walk right beside Ashleigh. No running around the paddock and getting the yearlings all worked up."

"Promise!" Rory said.

Ashleigh knew Rory would keep his promise, too. They'd all had it drilled into their heads how valuable these yearlings were.

On average, a yearling could sell for between twenty and seventy thousand dollars. There were exceptions if the yearling had royal breeding—like Wanderer's current yearling who was a grandson of Alydar, one of the best performing sires of the last decade. Slammer, as the kids had nicknamed the colt, had spirit, good conformation, and intelligence. Plus, his older sister, Quest, had won a Grade 1 race that day. Slammer was sure to sell for a high price at auction.

After dinner, Ashleigh returned to the barn to check on Lightning and spend some time with her. Rory tagged along.

"If you get to keep Lightning, Ash," he asked, "do you think Mom and Dad would let me have Moe?" Moe was the pony the Griffens had inherited with the farm.

"Moe belongs to all of us, but if I get to keep Lightning, Moe can be your special pony."

Rory grinned. "I think I'll go say good-night to him." Rory hurried to Moe's stall and let himself in. The five-year-old wasn't allowed to enter any of the other stalls alone, but Moe was laid-back and wouldn't harm a fly.

Ashleigh walked on to Lightning's stall. The mare had heard her voice and was already nickering a happy greeting. She walked to the half-door and stuck her nose against the bars. Ashleigh stopped outside the stall to take some treats from the tack box in the aisle.

"Yes, I'm coming," Ashleigh said. "Don't be so impatient. I've got your dessert. Back up a little so that I can get in."

Ashleigh squeezed into the stall to see Lightning standing with her ears pricked alertly as she watched Ashleigh, and more particularly, the carrot treats in Ashleigh's hand.

Ashleigh broke off a piece of carrot and offered it to the mare on the palm of her hand. Lightning lipped it up and began to chew, making loud crunching sounds.

"I've been thinking a lot about you," Ashleigh said, leaning her shoulder against the mare. "The humane society told my parents today that they still haven't decided whether we can adopt you or not. My parents said it was all bureaucratic stuff—whatever that means—but it scares me. You couldn't have a better home! Why don't they understand that and let us adopt you?"

Ashleigh scowled as she rubbed a hand over Lightning's velvety nose. "I don't know what I'd do if they took you away. I wish they didn't have control over who adopts you. But in a way, they helped save you, too. My parents said that you could never have been taken away from Mr. Nasty forever without the humane society helping with the legal stuff." Ashleigh laid her head against Lightning's neck. "But I still feel like *I* saved you. Why should they be the ones to decide where you'll live? It's not fair!"

Lightning whoofed a carroty breath through her nostrils, and turned her head to touch her nose against Ashleigh's arm. Ashleigh smiled and gently ran a hand over the mare's muzzle.

"So what should we do tomorrow? Practice more on the longe line, or maybe let you get the feel of a saddle on your back? I can't wait until I can ride you on the trails." Ashleigh tightened her arms around the mare's neck and kissed her.

"She's looking good," a voice called over the stall door. Ashleigh jumped. She hadn't heard anyone coming down the aisle. She turned her head to see Kurt.

"Sorry, I didn't mean to startle you," he said.

She smiled. "That's okay. I was just thinking about what I was going to do next with Lightning."

"Well, if you need any help, let me know," Kurt said.

Ashleigh hesitated for a second. "The humane society people were here today, and they still haven't decided whether we can adopt Lightning. I just don't get it—what's there to decide?"

Kurt frowned. He seemed to be considering his words. "Well, they may have been approached by other people who want to adopt Lightning."

"Really? How do you know?" Ashleigh said, shocked.

"Her story was written up in the local newspapers. I'm sure it stirred up a lot of sympathetic interest."

Ashleigh felt her heart sink. "Why didn't my parents say anything about this?" Ashleigh asked, bewildered.

"It's too soon to jump to conclusions," Kurt said quickly, seeing the expression on Ashleigh's face. "I know how attached you are to Lightning. Considering the excellent care and attention you've given her, the society may very well decide to let her stay here. If it makes you feel any better, I'm on your side." Kurt paused. "Anyway, we've got a long day with the year-lings ahead of us tomorrow. I'm going to turn in. Good-night, Ashleigh."

"Good-night, Kurt," Ashleigh called. She closed Lightning's stall door and leaned over it, watching as the white horse peacefully munched her hay. *Could someone else really adopt Lightning?* It didn't seem possible.

Ashleigh left the barn and went to her room. It was empty—Caroline was downstairs watching television with the rest of the family. Ashleigh sat down on the edge of her bed. Thankfully it was Saturday night, and she didn't have to do her homework. She would never have been able to concentrate on it anyway. Suddenly, she thought of her diary. She hadn't written in it much lately, but she felt like she needed to tonight. She took it out of her desk drawer, curled up on her bed, and began to write.

Dear Diary,

I was so excited about Lightning staying here at Edgardale, but now I don't know what to think. Some women from the humane society were here today to talk to Mom and Dad. I'm not really sure what they said. All I know is they haven't said we can adopt Lightning yet. I just don't see why they would have any problem letting her stay here. She looks so good now and she's really happy. I love her so much. Why would they want to take her away from me? I just feel so sad. My parents said there's nothing we can do, except wait. I hope they decide something soon. I hate waiting. Mona and I were just talking about how cool it would be if she got her horse for Christmas, like her parents have been hinting they'd get her, and I got Lightning. I really thought that might happen, but now I'm not so sure.

Ashleigh felt tears welling up in her eyes, and she tried blink them back. She'd always known that helping Lightning was a *good* thing. So why wasn't she being rewarded?

Anyway, I'm not going to give up yet. I'm going to keep working with Lightning and hope that she's staying right here. I want to ride her, soon!! And I won't do that if I stop trying with her. Hopefully, I will ride her, and I'll keep riding her forever and ever.

When Ashleigh put down her pen and closed the diary, she felt better—not good, but not quite so hopeless. She checked the clock and decided it wasn't too late to call Mona.

"They can't do that to do you!" Mona cried after Ashleigh told her friend about the visitors from the humane society and what Kurt had said. "I'm sure it's not true that someone else wants Lightning. It would be totally unfair. We've got to make sure they let you keep her."

"But how?" Ashleigh moaned.

"Well, Kurt's on your side, and so are your parents, so that's good. But don't you dare give up, Ashleigh Griffen. Now you'll really have to show them how perfect you and Lightning are together. Are you going to work her tomorrow?"

"I was going to . . . Yes, yes of course I am!" Ashleigh said, determined to get rid of her doubt.

"Why don't you ask Kurt or your parents to invite the humane society people to watch?" Mona suggested.

"Good idea, Mona," Ashleigh said excitedly. All she needed was a chance to show that she and Lightning were meant for each other.

"And I'll come over, too," Mona added. "Should I bring Silver so we can ride the ponies afterward?"

"That would be great. Thanks, Mona. See you tomorrow." Ashleigh felt much better. Mona was right. If the people from the humane society saw her working with Lightning, they might be convinced that Lightning should stay with her for good. She rushed downstairs to tell her parents Mona's plan.

3

Mona arrived on Silver after Ashleigh had finished her morning chores and was leading Lightning out of the barn.

"Just in time," Ashleigh called. "The humane society people will be here soon. You can untack Silver and put him in with Moe until I'm done with Lightning. Hey, and guess what?"

"What?" Mona asked, sliding down from Silver's back.

"Kurt said we could try Lightning under saddle!"

Ashleigh's parents had arranged for some people from the humane society to come watch Ashleigh work with Lightning. The Griffens were too busy to come and watch themselves, but Kurt had promised to be there to help. He explained how Ashleigh should start out and that he would join them once he had greeted the humane society visitors.

Before she led Lightning out of the barn, Ashleigh had brought out a saddle pad and one of her parents' old riding saddles, according to Kurt's instructions. Moe's saddle was much too small for Lightning. Ashleigh led the mare into the paddock. Lightning lifted her head, sniffed the air, then answered the whinny of one of the mares in a nearby paddock.

Ashleigh began by walking Lightning around the pasture as she usually did, then she worked her on the longe line for several minutes in both directions. She led Lightning over to where Mona was standing near the paddock fence.

"She looks better every day," Mona said.

"Thanks, but now comes the bigger test. Can you hand me that saddle pad?"

Mona did. It was fluffy and white and weighed very little. Ashleigh took the pad in one hand and held Lightning's lead in the other. Then she carefully laid the pad on Lightning's back. The mare's muscles quivered, but she'd been used to having a harness around her shoulders, and the pad weighed much less. Ashleigh began walking the mare in a large circle with the pad on her back. Lightning didn't seem to mind. So far, so good.

Just then, the same fancy gray car Ashleigh had seen before pulled up to the barn. Ashleigh tried to keep concentrating on Lightning, but out of the corner of her eye she saw two women step out of the car and look up at her. Kurt came out of the barn to greet them, and they stood talking and watching Ashleigh. They didn't appear to want to come any closer.

Suddenly Ashleigh felt nervous—as if the humane society would decide to take Lightning away the minute she made one mistake. But Ashleigh didn't want to make Lightning nervous, too. That would ruin everything. She decided to continue what she was doing and pretend they weren't there.

Once again, she brought Lightning to the paddock fence. "Did you see, Mona?" Ashleigh noted to her friend. "They're watching."

Mona nodded. "Don't let it bother you," she said. "Focus on Lightning."

"Can you hold her, while I get the saddle?" Ashleigh asked.

Mona took the lead shank in hand, and Ashleigh collected the saddle. Then she walked cautiously to the mare's head with the saddle in her arms. Ashleigh had thought Kurt would be there with her, and she felt nervous about trying to saddle Lightning on her own. But Kurt had told her what to do and she was confident Lightning would cooperate. She stopped in front of Lightning and let the mare sniff and examine the saddle. Without rushing, Ashleigh walked around Mona to Lightning's side and carefully lifted the saddle. Since Lightning stood a little over fifteen hands at her withers, Ashleigh had to stretch her arms before gently lowering the saddle toward the mare's back.

"Keep a good hold on her and be prepared," Ashleigh whispered to Mona, letting the saddle come to rest on Lightning's back. For an instant the mare froze, then she craned her head around to see what was on her back. Ashleigh knew that an unschooled horse's instinct was to buck off any foreign object from its back. It was an instinct going back to their days in the wild when pouncing predators were frequently a threat.

No one knew whether Lightning had ever been ridden or not. There was a chance that she never had a saddle on her back in her life. It was also possible that she had been schooled under saddle a long time ago and once she remembered the feeling of wearing a saddle, she would just take it all in stride. But even if Lightning knew perfectly well what a saddle was, she obviously hadn't been ridden for a very long time. She was still frightened and skittish after being so badly abused by her previous owner and she might try to buck.

Ashleigh quickly rubbed a hand down Lightning's

neck and spoke soothingly. "It's okay, girl. It's okay. I'm here, and I'd never do anything to hurt you." Lightning seemed to relax a little, but Ashleigh could sense the mare's uncertainty. "Let's walk forward a couple of steps." Mona led the mare forward as Ashleigh walked behind, keeping a soothing hand on Lightning's neck. For a few seconds everything was fine, then Lightning became uneasy with the weight on her back, did a quick sidestep, and the saddle fell to the ground.

This isn't going well, Ashleigh thought nervously. She glanced toward the barn self-consciously. The people from the humane society were standing there, and they were looking right at her.

She hadn't attached the girth, so there had been nothing to hold the saddle in place. Mona held Lightning while Ashleigh picked the saddle up off the ground. She spoke soothing words, and then let Lightning sniff the saddle again.

Then a voice spoke quietly from the paddock rail. It was Kurt. Ashleigh was relieved he was there to help.

"Ashleigh, since she knows you better, why don't you lead her and let Mona hold the saddle," Kurt instructed. "No offense, Mona, but the mare's been around Ashleigh more, and if she can see Ashleigh, she might feel more reassured."

"You're right," Mona said, not the least offended. "She does know Ashleigh better, and she keeps looking back to make sure Ash is still there."

The two girls changed places and tried again. This time, Ashleigh comforted and reassured Lightning face-to-face, while Mona lowered the saddle onto her back. Ashleigh felt Lightning stiffen up when the saddle touched her, but she continued to speak soothingly. The mare's ears flicked forward, listening to Ashleigh's voice, then flicked back in uncertainty. Lightning could no longer see the saddle, yet she felt its weight and it made her uneasy. Without warning, she swung her hindquarters around, and sent the saddle flying to the ground again.

Kurt picked up the saddle and they tried again. "Go forward slowly," Kurt said. "Keep talking to her. Just a couple of steps."

Ashleigh did as he said. Lightning hesitated, then walked forward. Her ears were still flicking back and forth like crazy, signaling her uncertainty, but finally her trust in Ashleigh won out. The mare walked a few steps forward, then a few more.

Then, suddenly, a bird flew too close overhead, and Lightning shied violently, sliding the saddle from her back. Ashleigh was glad it was an old saddle, because it was definitely taking a beating. She knew Lightning wasn't misbehaving deliberately—she was only frightened—but Ashleigh was getting discouraged. The people from the humane society were still watching from near the barn, leaning against their fancy gray car.

"Let me help," Kurt said, entering the paddock and approaching quietly so the mare wouldn't be startled. Kurt picked up the saddle and quietly instructed the girls, "Mona, go around to her other side. Ashleigh, stay where you are. When I lift the saddle onto her back, Mona, I want you to gently take hold of the stirrup leather." Ashleigh hadn't removed the stirrups from the saddle, but she had run up the irons so that they were securely tucked under the saddle flap and wouldn't fall free and bang into the mare's sides.

"I'll do the same on this side," Kurt continued. "I don't want you to put any downward pressure on the stirrup leather. The object is to hold the saddle in the center of her back and stop it from sliding if she shies again."

They got the saddle in place once more. "Okay," Kurt urged, "Ashleigh, walk her forward again. Keep talking quietly. Keep her concentrated on you and your voice. Her ears should stay pricked forward," he advised.

Ashleigh was distracted by the sight of the gray car pulling out of the drive. The people from the humane society had left. They hadn't stayed more than fifteen minutes. It was as if they weren't even giving her a chance. Ashleigh took a deep breath.

"Okay, girl," Ashleigh said softly, "let's try it again. You can do it, and you know I wouldn't do anything to hurt you. Come on, just a couple of steps."

Still, Lightning seemed uneasy, but at least her ears remained forward, listening to Ashleigh's voice. She took a step, then another, then another. Kurt and Mona walked along at the mare's sides, in order to steady the saddle if it slipped.

"Keep her going," Kurt whispered to Ashleigh. "Take her in a big circle."

Ashleigh led Lightning without incident through a circle. Kurt motioned her to try another; then yet another. Only then, did he nod and smile. "I think we got her past the worst fear. That's enough for today. We can try the girth another day. It's best to end it on a good note."

Ashleigh and Mona were both smiling at their success. Ashleigh felt a huge wave of relief pass over her. Lightning could do it—she just needed a lot of time and patience.

"I just wish those women from the humane society had seen how well she went at the end," she said wistfully.

Kurt frowned. "Never mind them, let's just concentrate on Lightning," he said. "I know you hoped you'd be riding her by now. And with another horse," Kurt went on, lifting the saddle from Lightning's back and patting the mare, "you could try to take the next step now, but she's had too traumatic a past. She needs to take it slow, otherwise you could turn her off altogether."

Ashleigh was anxious to take the next step and introduce the girth, but considering Lightning's reactions that day, she knew Kurt was right. Any training had to be slow and easy with Lightning. She had a lot of bad memories to overcome, and Ashleigh knew that horses had *long* memories, especially of physical pain. Riding Lightning would just have to wait.

After they'd released Lightning in the paddock to graze to her heart's content, Ashleigh set off to catch Moe. The pony hated being caught, but once he knew he had to work, he was enthusiastic and cooperative. Finally, Ashleigh and Mona had their ponies saddled up and they set off up the grassy lanes that divided the Edgardale paddocks.

Ashleigh should have felt better about all the progress they had made with Lightning in just one day, but her mind was flooded with worry. The humane society hadn't seen the good part, only the bad. After what they'd seen—Lightning shying and dumping the saddle on the ground—would they think Ashleigh couldn't handle her?

The lanes and paddocks eventually led up a low hill to the woods behind Edgardale where the girls had gotten lost during the spring and had stumbled upon Lightning. But Mona and Ashleigh weren't interested in exploring the woods. They only wanted to canter up and down the lanes and enjoy themselves, especially now that the days of oppressive summer heat were gone. Ashleigh really felt like she needed a good canter to forget everything.

Mona's pony, Silver, was a purebred Welsh and slightly bigger than Moe, who everyone had decided was a Shetland-Welsh mix. Moe had come with the farm, so no one knew his true background. Silver, being longer-legged, could cover the straights faster, but Moe had more maneuverability on short turns, and could whip around them and be on his way before Silver was even halfway through the turn. The girls usually ended up coming close to a tie in their unofficial races. This time, Ashleigh let Moe go flat out around a turn in the lane, just ahead of Mona.

"Okay, you beat us this time, Ash," Mona said, breathlessly, "but wait until you come over to my place and I put you through my jumping course. I'll be riding my new horse and you'll be riding Lightning!"

Ashleigh put up her hand and gave Mona a high-five. "Keep your fingers crossed, Mona!" she said.

As they rode home, Ashleigh wondered if she really ever would get to ride Lightning. It was beginning to look more and more unlikely.

4

"I can't believe it's auction day already!" Ashleigh exclaimed.

"I brought my camera," Mona said, "just in case we see any big stars!"

"Horse-stars or people-stars?" Caroline asked. She had been looking bored, staring out the window with a glazed expression, but she suddenly perked up at the mention of stars. Major horse sales inevitably drew celebrities from both the horse world and the entertainment world, and Caroline loved spotting celebrities.

Ashleigh's mother had picked them all up just after school and headed toward Lexington, the center of the racing industry and the home of Keeneland—where the most prestigious and lucrative Thoroughbred auctions in the country were held. Ashleigh had invited Mona to come with them to the Keeneland auction and Mona had been overjoyed. She'd been to the races there, but never the auction. Mr. Griffen had already gone on ahead with the farm's huge horse van, carrying Edgardale's eight yearlings that would be auctioned off in the next few days. Kurt had stayed behind to look after the horses at the farm.

They stopped off at a motel to unload their luggage and then Mrs. Griffen drove on to the backside of the track where the horses were stabled. The Griffens had already reserved their block of stalls for their yearlings, and they all headed in that direction. The backside was alive with activity. Hundreds of horses were there to be auctioned, but the auction was part of Keeneland's racing season, so a lot of top racehorses were stabled there for the season, too. Trainers, grooms, stable hands, owners, and prospective buyers crowded the shed rows.

Ashleigh loved the hustle and bustle and the sight of so many beautiful horses, all in peak condition and lovingly cared for. There were the smells, too, of hay and leather and horse. Keeneland was a beautiful track with landscaped grounds that extended into the backside. Baskets of flowers hung from the eves of the barns and the lawns were freshly mowed. Many other racing facilities were in decline and looked neglected, but Keeneland had flourished.

"This is great," Mona said excitedly to Ashleigh.

"I've never been on the backside here before. And look at these horses!"

"Pretty incredible." Ashleigh said, stepping aside to allow a groom leading an elegant bay colt to pass.

They soon found Mr. Griffen who was talking with one of Keeneland's stable staff.

"The yearlings are all bedded down for the night, but I'm going to need everyone's help tomorrow and the next day, getting them ready for the auction ring," he said.

Caroline didn't look too pleased at the prospect, but Ashleigh and Mona nodded happily, eager to be involved. Each of the yearlings had to be impeccably groomed before they went into the ring.

"Why don't you kids take a tour around the barns while we finish up some paperwork," Mrs. Griffen suggested. "But please stay together and keep an eye on Rory."

"Okay, Mom," Ashleigh replied.

Caroline brightened up at the prospect of a tour, and took Rory's hand as they started down the shed row. "I wonder if anybody famous is here yet?" she mused.

"I'd rather see some famous horses," Mona said. "Do you know if any top horses are stabled on the grounds now?" she asked Ashleigh.

Ashleigh shook her head. "I was hoping Wanderer's Quest would be racing here this season, and we could visit her, but the Fontaines ran her at Belmont instead. Which was just fine, since she won," Ashleigh added.

"It's still cool, even if we don't see the big guys," Mona said excitedly.

There were so many top-class horses—some with legendary sires and dams—Ashleigh was awestruck. Some of the highly strung yearlings were pacing their stalls nervously, while others were being walked under the shady trees or allowed to graze in the grassy areas near the barns.

They'd only covered half the barn area when Caroline checked her watch. "We'd better head back," she told the others. "We've been gone for nearly an hour."

Ashleigh was reluctant to turn back, but Ashleigh could see that Rory was getting tired. It had been a long walk for his five-year-old legs. "Want to ride piggyback for a while, Rory?" she asked.

His face lit up as he nodded, and Ashleigh knelt down so he could climb up on her shoulders. "I'll pretend you're my horse," he said giggling. "Giddyup, horse. Faster!"

Ashleigh managed to jog along with him for a while, but Rory wasn't as light as he used to be, and she soon slowed down to a walk. She was getting tired, too. It had been a long and busy day.

Back at their motel, Ashleigh had trouble sleeping. She knew she needed a good night's sleep and would have to be up very early for the auction, but her mind was racing. Being at Keeneland was a thrill, but as she finally drifted off, her last thoughts were of Lightning home at Edgardale, not the auction.

Ashleigh walked up the well-worn path to Lightning's paddock. She would groom the mare quickly, longe her, and then give her a nice hot bubble bath when they were finished working. Lightning would love that. But the gate was standing open and the paddock was empty. Ashleigh froze in panic. Had Lightning gotten loose somehow? She ran back to the barn and rushed to Lightning's stall, but the mare wasn't there. Had the humane society come and taken her away?!

Ashleigh woke with a start. She was relieved to discover that she was only having a bad dream, but her heart was still racing. *Was Lightning okay? Was Kurt keeping an eye on her? Stupid questions,* Ashleigh thought, as she began to drift off again. *Of course, he was. But had the humane society made any decisions? Had they come to the farm while she was gone?*

The next thing Ashleigh knew, there was a loud hammering on the motel room door. "Rise and shine," Mr. Griffen called. Caroline groaned and pulled the blanket over her head, but Ashleigh and Mona sat up in bed, then looked at each other and grinned. A half hour later, the girls were showered and dressed, and Caroline was finally pulling herself out of bed. "Save me some breakfast," she called as the girls left the room.

By six o'clock they were at the track and tending to the yearlings. They weren't alone. The backside was already in full-swing, with horses being walked, stalls being cleaned, owners and owners' representatives inspecting their charges. A groom walked by leading a horse. It was a beautiful white mare with a gentle expression and long, flowing mane and tail that reminded Ashleigh so much of Lightning that she almost gasped. Like Lightning, she was obviously a mature horse, since she'd lost the gray dapples that characterized white horses in their early years. At one point, Lightning would have been a dappled gray, too.

She nudged Mona and pointed to the mare. "Wow," Mona said. "She looks like she could be Lightning's sister."

Ashleigh nodded. "Except that Lightning's not a full Thoroughbred, and that mare would have to be if she's being auctioned here." Ashleigh sighed. "It makes me miss Lightning."

"Kurt is taking good care of her," Mona reassured her friend.

"Hey, you two," Mr. Griffen called to them teasingly. "Are you going to get any work done today or what?"

"Right, Dad," Ashleigh said.

Ashleigh, Caroline, and Mona cleaned three stalls while the older Griffens and Rory led out three of the yearlings. Once the stalls were clean and the three yearlings were back in place, Ashleigh, Caroline, and Mona walked out three more yearling while the Griffens cleaned their stalls. Ashleigh's parents believed in an equal assignment of duties. No one got stuck doing all the unpleasant work. Ashleigh and the others were so used to the routine of mucking out by now that they didn't question it.

Go Gen's filly, Zip Away's colt, and Althea's colt would go into the auction ring that day. The auction was held in the sales pavilion, with an elevated walk-out stage for the horses just in front of the auctioneer's stand. There were ample seats for the prospective buyers set in a semi-circle around the walkout stage.

Ashleigh and Mona began grooming Go Gen's filly, a chestnut with a wide blaze and four white stockings. She was an easygoing yearling that the kids had nicknamed Honey. She stood patiently as they took her out of her stall and bathed her, walked her in the sunshine and rubbed her coat with towels until she was dry, and then set to work on her coat, mane, and tail with various grooming tools. They used clippers to carefully trim the long hairs inside her ears and hoof oil to make her hoofs shine. By the time they were finished, the filly looked like a beauty queen, her coat glimmering like a new penny; her mane and tail tangle-free and wafting in the breeze. They covered the filly with a light sheet and returned her to her stall.

Zip Away's colt, Tumble, was more of a problem. He loved to roll, and had done a lot of rolling in his stall the night before. His mane and tail were tangled with bits of bedding and would require a lot of combing to get rid of the mess.

In the next stall Caroline, Mrs. Griffen, and Rory worked on the last colt. Rory was sometimes more a hindrance than a help. "No, Rory, you cannot give him any more carrots," Ashleigh heard her mother call. "He needs grooming right now, not feeding. Take a brush and go over his legs."

Ashleigh looked at Mona and chuckled. They were diligently working combs through Tumble's wispy mane and tail, trying desperately to get all the tangles out of his tail and make his mane lie flat. He stood chomping his hay, enjoying every minute of the extra attention.

"Ash," Mona asked, "aren't you starting to feel kind of sad that these guys will be going to other owners today? I know I am."

"I always feel sad," Ashleigh said. "The auction is pretty exciting and all of that, but I know I'll miss them. It's just that my parents couldn't make any money if they didn't sell our yearlings." As she spoke, Ashleigh felt a pang, remembering that she might soon have to give up another horse, too, and one that meant even more to her. She was trying to keep her mind on the auction, but she found that Lightning was never far from her thoughts.

They continued to work together as a team when the auction began. Go Gen's filly, Honey, would be their first yearling to be auctioned, and she now had a number, appropriately called a hip number, glued to her upper hip. Ashleigh and Mr. Griffen held her in line as the first yearlings went off. Then their turn came, and Mr. Griffen handed off the filly to one of the auction handlers, who led her on-stage in front of a crowded pavilion. The auctioneer reviewed her pedigree, which was printed in all the programs, as the handler walked the filly in a circle so the audience could see her movement. It was thrilling and nerve-wracking for Ashleigh to stand there with her father as Honey—a filly who's birth she had witnessed—was looked over by thousands of critical eyes. One day Ashleigh hoped to be in the audience, bidding on horses for her own Thoroughbred farm.

"Shall we start the bidding . . ." the auctioneer called.

Ashleigh had only minimal knowledge of what their horses should bring at auction, so she watched her father's expressions as the bids rose. He frowned at one point when the bidding seemed to stall, but then a new interest came in. Finally, the bidding closed and the auctioneer banged down his gavel. "Sold!" Ashleigh saw that her father was smiling, and she felt relieved. Honey had done well.

Next, Mrs. Griffen, Caroline, and Mona brought up Tumble, who was getting fractious with all the noise and confusion of the crowds.

"Looks like they've got their hands full," Mr. Griffen said worriedly as they walked by, headed toward the auction ring.

"Good job you two!" Ashleigh's mother called out to them, as they led Tumble off to the auction ring. "Don't worry—we're fine—we ladies can handle him!"

Ashleigh helped her father put Honey away and then rushed back to see the bidding for Tumble. She watched as the feisty colt tugged on the auction handler's lead, pawed the dirt, and snorted at the crowd. Tumble looked like he would be a handful, but he also looked every bit the champion that his bloodlines promised he would be. The bidding rose despite his antics. When the gavel went down, Tumble gave a little buck.

Ashleigh went to join her father, who was waiting by the ring with Edgardale's next yearling. He looked pleased. "That went better than I thought," he said happily.

The last yearling auctioned that day had very good, but unspectacular sire- and dam-lines. Ashleigh knew from her parents' expressions that the horse had sold for less then they had expected.

"They're disappointed," Mona whispered to Ashleigh.

"Yeah, they are, but the others did well, and we still

have Slammer, Wanderer's colt, going off tomorrow. He'll do well, don't worry," Ashleigh said confidently.

The rest of the day was spent getting the sold year-lings off to their new homes and preparing for the next important auction day. When their chores were done, Ashleigh and Mona wandered the backside, on the lookout for famous jockeys and trainers.

Ashleigh noticed a group of reporters and camera-men crowded around one of the stalls. When she and Mona went closer they saw it was Rudy Greene—the famous young jockey who had won the Kentucky Derby that May—and Tough Love, the gorgeous liver chestnut he had won it on.

"Go and ask him for his autograph," Mona dared Ashleigh. They were both staring, completely starstruck.

"No way," Ashleigh said. "You do it." Just then Rudy Greene looked up.

"Ash, he's looking right at us!" Mona gasped. She grabbed Ashleigh's arm and they quickly walked away, trying to maintain their composure.

Ashleigh would have liked to get Rudy Greene's autograph, but she still felt lucky. It wasn't every day she got to see such a famous jockey and horse team. If it wasn't for Lightning waiting for her at home, Ashleigh would have wished she could stay longer at

Keeneland. She loved the excitement of the track. She and Mona roamed around for hours until they headed back to the motel.

When Slammer came out the next day, there were ohs and ahs of admiration from the audience. Ashleigh looked on proudly. He was a magnificent looking yearling, standing close to fifteen hands, and he was nowhere near full-grown. Ashleigh guessed he would grow another four inches at his shoulder, putting him closer to sixteen or possibly seventeen hands. Muscles rippled under his black coat. He had personality, too, like all of Wanderer's foals. Slammer was full of himself and flirted with the audience—eyeing them, arching his neck, prancing on the platform without appearing wild or uncontrolled.

The bidding started high and kept going up. Ashleigh and her family watched from behind the auctioneer's stand, gasping as the bidding kept rising. Mona clutched Ashleigh's elbow, her mouth open in amazement.

From where they stood, they couldn't see the audience, but they could see the board. When the auctioneer called "SOLD!" Slammer had gone for more than twice the price the Griffens had expected: two hundred thousand dollars. It was a breathtaking amount of money.

Ashleigh looked at her parents. Their mouths were gaping open in amazement. Ashleigh recognized some other Thoroughbred breeders from their area making their way through the crowd to congratulate her parents and she overheard their excited talk. The Griffens had just reached the highest price of any yearling they had ever sold! And their mare, Wanderer, had just increased her foal crop's value by fifty percent.

Ashleigh knew her parents must be thrilled, and she ought to be, too. But she would be sad to see Slammer go, and his sale marked the end of the auction for them. This afternoon they would return to Edgardale. She couldn't wait to see Lightning again, but at the same time she was almost dreading having to face up to what the humane society would decide to do.

It was mid-afternoon when Mrs. Griffen pulled into Edgardale's drive after dropping off Mona. The late fall days were growing shorter, and already the trees were casting the long shadows of dusk. As soon as the car came to a stop, Ashleigh jumped out and raced in the direction of the paddocks. Now that they were home, she just had to see Lightning.

As she dashed across the yard, she saw that the same gray car had pulled in and parked near the barn. The people from the humane society were here again! Ashleigh zoomed around the end of the barn and had a clear view of Lightning's paddock. Two women stood with Kurt near Lightning's paddock fence. It looked like the same two women who had come to Edgardale the last time. They were all watching Lightning, who was looking gorgeous as she grazed peacefully. The women were talking quickly to each other, but Kurt seemed to be keeping silent.

Ashleigh felt a strange twinge in her stomach. *What are these two women doing, coming to Edgardale without any warning to inspect* my *horse?* As Ashleigh walked up behind them, they continued talking, unaware of her presence. Both women looked dressed up to go out to dinner, not to visit a farm. Kurt saw Ashleigh, though, and said something to the women. Ashleigh couldn't hear him, but the women suddenly turned around and smiled at her.

"Hello, there. You must be Ashleigh. Mr. Bradley has been telling us how much you've contributed to this mare's rehabilitation," the one with a black fur-trimmed coat and leather boots said. "By the way, I'm Lila Cotswald, and this is Anne Walker," she went on. "We're patrons of the humane society, and we were just admiring how well the mare is doing," she said in a sugary voice.

Ashleigh didn't know what to say, so she only nodded.

"Well, we certainly appreciate your hard work," Anne Walker said. She was wearing high heels and was gripping the paddock fence to keep from toppling over.

Lightning had noticed that Ashleigh was there now, too, and she came trotting across the pasture to greet her. "Hi, sweetie," Ashleigh called to the mare. "Did you miss me? I've got your treats."

Lightning eagerly stuck her head over the paddock fence, and Ashleigh fed her slices of apple.

"You've been around horses all your life?" Anne Walker asked.

"Yes," said Ashleigh, feeding Lightning another apple.

"You have a lot of beautiful horses on this farm to work with every day," she continued.

Ashleigh nodded, feeling a growing lump in her stomach and wondering where the conversation was leading. *Just what is she implying?*

"You have a wonderful way with horses," Lila Cotswald said. "This one seems to really trust you."

Ashleigh was glad that they had noticed how happy

Lightning had been to see her. "I love all of the horses," Ashleigh answered. "But Lightning is really special. I mean I helped rescue her. I'm going to start riding her soon, too."

"So she's well enough to be ridden?" Anne Walker asked, turning to Kurt.

"The mare has been brought up to condition gradually," Kurt explained. "Riding her in a few weeks shouldn't be a problem, and it certainly won't hurt her."

"Oh, I see," Anne Walker said hastily. She exchanged a look with her companion.

"Well, we'll be back in touch. The six-month waiting period before adoption ends soon, and we'll certainly keep you apprised of developments," Lila Cotswald said vaguely. Both women smiled at Ashleigh. "Keep up the good work."

"Thanks," Ashleigh said, smiling weakly, "I will."

Then the two women headed back to their sleek gray car and drove off.

Ashleigh looked at Kurt, shaking her head. "I don't understand. What do they mean, 'apprised of developments'?"

"I'm not sure I know myself," Kurt answered. Ashleigh saw that he was frowning.

5

Ashleigh awoke the next morning with a very foggy brain. She'd been tossing and turning all night, worrying feverishly about Lightning, thinking about what the two women had said. She could barely pull herself out of bed when her alarm went off. But then the thought that her days with Lightning might be numbered got her dressed and out to the barn for her morning chores in a hurry.

Mona was equally tired when they met on the bus. After getting home from the auction, she'd gone shopping with her mother at the only mall in the area, which was an hour's drive east. "All the stores were decorated for Christmas already," Mona said. "It really put me in the Christmas mood. I just hope I get that horse!"

Ashleigh wished she could say the same. Normally, she got really excited over Christmas, but this year she had other things on her mind. She told Mona about the visitors from the humane society.

"So, what did they want?" Mona asked. "What did they say?"

"They thought Lightning looked good and they thanked me for taking such good care of her. They told Kurt and me that they'd 'keep us apprised of developments,' whatever that means."

"It wouldn't make sense for them to send her somewhere else," Mona protested. "At least it sounds like they're giving you a fair shot."

Ashleigh shrugged. She didn't know what to think anymore.

Ashleigh knew she had to try to lighten up. Worrying wasn't going to help matters. "Can you come by today after school, Mona?" she asked. "Kurt wants to try her under saddle again."

"I wouldn't miss it!"

"Nice and easy," Kurt said to Ashleigh. He stood at Lightning's head, holding her halter as Ashleigh buckled the girth for the first time. "Not too tight," he warned. "You don't want to pinch her."

Ashleigh carefully fastened the second buckle, remaining alert for Lightning's reaction. Lightning had become accustomed to the saddle on her back, but Ashleigh knew that some horses didn't like the girth tightening process and would swing around and try to bite. Jolita, usually a placid mare, tried to bite whenever Ashleigh's parents saddled her for a ride. Of course, they only rode the broodmares during the months when they weren't heavily pregnant, and then only for light exercise.

So far Lightning had only flicked her ears back and forth between Kurt and Ashleigh. Ashleigh left the girth loose enough that she could easily slip a finger between it and Lightning's side.

"That's my girl," Ashleigh said, laying a hand on Lightning's neck.

"Okay," Kurt instructed, "step back and I'll lead her forward. You don't want to be standing too close in case she kicks out."

Ashleigh stepped a few feet back and crossed her fingers behind her back, praying that Lightning would walk calmly on behind Kurt despite the tight girth.

Kurt coaxed Lightning forward. "Come on, girl," he said quietly as he put pressure on the lead shank. For a moment she balked, bracing her legs and flicking her ears nervously. Kurt released pressure on the lead and spoke soothingly. When the mare relaxed, he tried to lead her forward again.

Ashleigh let out a sigh of relief when Lightning took one hesitant step, then another. She saw Kurt begin to smile, but his attention was still concentrated on the mare. "See, there's nothing to be afraid of," he said to her. He led her in a circle around the paddock. With each step Lightning seemed less hesitant, as if she was remembering past experiences with a saddle on her back, and knew that this thing tied around her belly wasn't going to hurt her.

After two full circles, Kurt called quietly to Ashleigh, "Bring me the longe line."

Ashleigh ran to get it.

"Let me try her the first time," Kurt said. "If she seems to be moving all right, then you can take a turn. I know you're dying to." He flashed a grin at Ashleigh.

Ashleigh knew he was being cautious. Neither of them expected that Lightning would deliberately hurt Ashleigh, but if the mare suddenly got upset, Kurt was better prepared to control her.

"You're doing good, Lightning," Ashleigh praised as she handed Kurt the longe line, which he clipped to the mare's halter. Ashleigh joined Mona at the end of the paddock as Kurt stepped back and gradually let the longe line out. When he was about ten feet away from Lightning, Kurt flicked the line. "Walk on, Lightning," he called.

Lightning knew the longeing procedure well by now and immediately walked forward. She began circling around Kurt.

"She's doing it," Ashleigh said, delighted with Lightning's progress. "Maybe she *was* trained to be ridden before Mr. Nasty got her," she said to Mona.

"So far, so good," Mona agreed with a smile. After Lightning had circled several times, with Kurt gradually letting out a few more feet of the longe line, Kurt called, "Let's see how she handles it at a trot." He flicked the line again and called, "Trot, Lightning. Trot on."

Lightning obediently increased her pace, but after half a circle at a trot, Ashleigh gulped. With the more jarring rhythm of the trot, the saddle had started to slip. The girth was too loose to hold it in place. Should the saddle slip too far down the mare's side, Ashleigh knew Lightning would definitely panic. But Kurt had seen the slipping saddle, too.

He reacted immediately, calling out, "Lightning, halt!"

The mare dropped back to a walk for a few strides, then stopped. The saddle remained precariously balanced halfway down Lightning's shoulder, and she didn't like it. Ashleigh could see her suddenly tense moves and knew Lightning was confused, frightened, and ready to take flight, as all horses instinctively did when they felt threatened.

"Go to her head," Kurt called to Ashleigh. "Hold her and try to calm her. I'll straighten the saddle."

Ashleigh walked toward Lightning, trying to appear calm in order to reassure her. Kurt slowly walked forward, too, keeping a grip on the longe line and shortening it as he walked toward Lightning.

Ashleigh called to the mare, "Easy, girl, easy." But she could see that Lightning didn't look at easy at all.

Don't panic, Ashleigh thought as she drew closer to the mare. Ashleigh knew Kurt had the longe line, so Lightning couldn't go far even if she bolted. Ashleigh was more concerned about Lightning's mental state if the slipping saddle spooked her. How long before she could regain the mare's trust again and eventually ride her?

Ashleigh reached Lightning's head. As soon as she saw the mare's eyes, she knew that she had less trust in Ashleigh than she ever had before. But Ashleigh reminded herself that Lightning had been badly abused. She was only frightened and acting on her instincts. If no harm came to her now or in any of their sessions together, Lightning would soon relax and begin to enjoy herself.

Rubbing a hand on Lightning's neck to distract her, Kurt quickly righted the saddle, then tightened the girth another notch before the mare knew what was happening. For an instant, Lightning flicked back her ears, but the saddle was still loose enough that the girth wasn't pinching.

"Okay, lead her forward," Kurt quietly instructed Ashleigh. "I'll stay right with you."

Ashleigh tugged gently on the lead. "Walk on, girl." The mare did, although her steps were more hesitant than before. The three of them continued around the paddock tentatively.

Then Kurt said, "Let me try her on the longe line again and then we'll quit on a good note."

Ashleigh nodded, handed Kurt the longe line, and returned to the fence.

Kurt urged Lightning through her paces again. This time the saddle stayed in place, and the mare circled at a walk and then a trot, stepping out confidently, without a mishap. After a few minutes, Kurt called Lightning to a halt, and gathered up the longe line. After patting her in approval, he led Lightning over to the girls, a wide grin creasing his face.

Ashleigh grinned back. "She did it!" she said, going to Lightning's head to pat her.

"That she did," Kurt replied. "Keep at it a little bit

every day until she's cantering circles, and before you know it, you'll be up there in her saddle."

"Thanks, Kurt. I wouldn't have known how to train her without your help, and my parents just don't have the time."

"Don't worry, I'm enjoying it," Kurt said. "Well, go get her untacked. And I think she deserves a treat."

Ashleigh was already digging in her pocket for carrots.

Every day after school, Ashleigh took Lightning out to the paddock to longe her under saddle. The late November days were growing cold, and Ashleigh had to bundle up in her parka. Within a week, Lightning was cantering circles on the longe line under tack, and Ashleigh was encouraged. When she was working with Lightning, Ashleigh almost forgot that she might not have the mare much longer. Their future would soon be decided for them. Ashleigh didn't want to think negative thoughts, but the best she could hope for was that she'd be able to ride Lightning herself at least once before the worst happened and the humane society took her away.

*   *   *

The holiday spirit was beginning to infect everyone. Mona and Ashleigh were members of the school choir, and had been practicing Christmas and Hanukkah songs during music period in preparation for the fifth grade's role in the winter assembly. Caro went out shopping with her friends every afternoon that she could, and was hiding away packages in their bedroom when she thought Ashleigh wouldn't notice. Ashleigh had known about all of Caro's hiding places for years, but this year the only Christmas gift Ashleigh wanted was Lightning. She had no desire to snoop.

6

Today I'm going to ride Lightning, Ashleigh thought as she opened her eyes on Saturday morning. She dressed quickly, gobbled up half a bowl of cereal, and raced out to the barn.

Outside, it was cold and bright. The broodmares' breaths hung in the air in frosty clouds. Ashleigh led Lightning out to the paddock where they always trained. Just then, Mona rode up on Silver. She was wearing a puffy, blue parka and a big scarf to keep out the cold. Ashleigh could barely see her face beneath her riding helmet.

"Hi, Ash," she called. "I'll be there in a minute—just as soon as I put Silver away."

Ashleigh was nervous as she brought Lightning's tack out of the barn. The mare had become accustomed to the saddle on her back, but this was the first time Ashleigh would actually try to ride her. *How will*

Lightning react with me up on her back, giving commands from there and not the ground?

Kurt and Mona came out to the paddock to help. Kurt had warned Ashleigh not to try mounting Lightning for the first time without him. Ashleigh wouldn't have risked that. She wanted Kurt there to help. He looked on as Mona held Lightning and Ashleigh tacked her up.

"Remember," he said to Ashleigh, "you're going to have to tighten the girth more than you did when you were only longeing. You don't want the saddle slipping when you put your weight into the stirrup."

Ashleigh nodded, adjusting the leather riding gloves on her hands, and fastening the chin strap on her riding helmet. She pulled the girth buckles one hole tighter. Lightning seemed happy with the tighter girth, but Ashleigh knew she would have to tighten it again once she was in the saddle. "Good girl," she murmured.

"She seems to be doing okay," Mona said, rubbing Lightning's nose.

Next, Ashleigh put on the bridle, looping the reins over Lightning's neck before removing her halter. Then she slid the bridle up the mare's head, gently pressing the bit between Lightning's teeth before bringing the headpiece up over her ears, and pulling her long white forelock free. She buckled the throat lash, leaving four fingers between it and Lightning's throat. Finally, she buckled the noseband, snug, but not too tight.

Lightning was ready to go. Ashleigh tried not to be nervous. She knew her feelings would be transmitted to Lightning directly through the reins.

"A couple of things to remember," Kurt advised. "All your moves should be easy and gentle, Ashleigh. After I give you a leg up, lower your weight gradually into the saddle. Don't startle her by suddenly sitting down hard. After you're in the saddle, we'll stand for a while to let her get used to your weight. Then I'll lead you a few steps forward. If she starts to get uneasy, don't tense up. She'll be reassured if you stay calm and relaxed and talk to her."

"What if she bucks?" Mona asked.

"Let's just hope she doesn't. I don't think she will at this point," Kurt said. "She knows and trusts Ashleigh too much by now. But this is still a new experience for her, so she will probably be skittish."

"I just want to make this as easy as I can for her," Ashleigh said. "She's been through so much awful and scary stuff. I don't want to do that to her again."

"We won't," Kurt firmly assured Ashleigh. "If she shows any hesitation or nervousness, we'll stop and wait for another day. Does that sound okay?"

Ashleigh nodded. She looked at Lightning, who was gazing at Ashleigh through her gentle brown eyes. Ashleigh felt like she was communicating with the mare, but she wasn't exactly sure what Lightning was telling her.

"Ready?" Kurt asked.

Ashleigh nodded again, feeling a lump in her stomach. She really wanted her first ride to go well and knew how disappointed she would be if it didn't. But she couldn't let herself think of anything going wrong.

Ashleigh stood at Lightning's side with Kurt. She smoothed her hand down Lightning's neck, then with Mona still holding Lightning's head, and Kurt standing behind her, Ashleigh reached up and gathered Lightning's reins with her left hand. Ashleigh bent her left leg and Kurt cupped her knee in his hands and lifted her up, so that her belly was resting on top of the saddle. Then, with one hand holding the reins at the base of Lightning's neck, and the other on the back of the saddle, she raised her right leg, lifting it gently over Lightning's back, then slowly and carefully, she lowered herself into the saddle. Lightning hadn't moved. It seemed like they were all holding their breath. Ashleigh slipped her feet into the stirrups. So far, so good.

When she had finally settled her full weight in the

saddle, Lightning snorted and craned her head around to get a better look at Ashleigh on her back.

"It's okay, Lightning," Ashleigh said. "It's only me sitting up here, and you know I love you."

The mare relaxed a little, but not completely.

"The girth has to come in another notch," Kurt said, "or the saddle's going to slip. Mona, keep holding her head. Ashleigh, just stay calm. Slide your leg forward so that I can tighten the girth."

Ashleigh did, moving her left leg in front of the saddle so that Kurt could lift the saddle flap and get to the girth buckles below. Lightning started as the girth grew tighter, but Ashleigh kept talking to her. "We're only doing this so the saddle won't slide, girl. You wouldn't like that at all." Lightning's ears flicked back as she listened to Ashleigh's voice.

"Okay," Kurt said, lowering the flap. Ashleigh slid her leg back into position and pushed her weight down into her heels. Kurt took Mona's place at Lightning's head. "Ask her to walk," he told Ashleigh.

Ashleigh tightened her legs slightly, keeping the reins loose. "Walk on," she commanded.

Lightning hesitated with her ears pinned back. She knew the command from her lessons on the longe line, but she seemed unsure now that there was someone on her back.

Again Ashleigh spoke soothingly, then squeezed her legs against Lightning's side. Kurt reinforced Ashleigh's aides by gently tugging on the base of the reins. Finally, Lightning moved forward without further protest. Slowly they walked a small circle in the paddock. Kurt remained at Lightning's head, but he no longer held her reins. Ashleigh sat deep in the saddle, getting a feel for the rhythm of the mare's gait. She could hardly believe it—she was riding Lightning!

After another circle, Kurt and Mona stepped away and told Ashleigh to keep the mare going on her own. With quiet hands and the gentle pressure of her legs when needed, Ashleigh kept Lightning walking on through the circle, then widened their course.

Ashleigh was gradually becoming more confident. She tried reining Lightning through more difficult moves, crossing the paddock on a diagonal and changing directions, turning the mare again in a figure eight. Kurt called to her to halt. "She looks relaxed. I bet she's done this before. Let's try the next step."

When Ashleigh stopped, Mona gave her a big smile and a thumbs-up from the paddock fence. "Looking good," she called.

"Thanks. I feel great!" Ashleigh replied, grinning from ear to ear.

Kurt walked up with the longe line and fastened it to Lightning's bridle. "Try her at a trot on the longe," he said. "She'll probably be fine, but I want to play it safe." He backed off and Ashleigh walked Lightning in a circle around him at the end of the long line.

"Okay," Kurt said. "When you're ready, trot on."

Ashleigh squeezed hard with her legs and urged, "Trot, Lightning." But the mare didn't change gaits, she only walked faster. Ashleigh persisted, pressing Lightning's sides lightly with both heels. "Trot on, girl," she called. Lightning responded, switching gaits and picking up the trot. Ashleigh began to post, checking her diagonal and rising in time with the mare's outside shoulder. They continued smoothly on the circle.

"Good," Kurt called. "She's moving easily."

"There we go," Ashleigh told the mare. "You're doing great. Keep it up. Good girl."

After several circles, Kurt told Ashleigh to pull the mare up. He removed the longe line. "Okay, try her on your own," he said, smiling up to Ashleigh. "Then we should probably call it quits for the day. We don't want to bombard her with too much in one session."

Ashleigh nodded and urged Lightning forward again. This time the mare broke eagerly into a trot when asked. Her ears flicked back toward Ashleigh, alert to every command. Ashleigh trotted her up to the end of the paddock, circled and came down the center line. She looked to the other end of the paddock where Kurt and Mona were standing. Her parents had come out of the barn to watch, too. Everyone was smiling.

Ashleigh felt her heart swell. It was like a dream come true. She was finally riding the beautiful mare she'd rescued. "You're the best, Lightning," Ashleigh murmured gently, brushing her knuckles against the mare's withers.

Lightning snorted softly as if she understood, and the two happily continued their course around the paddock, until Ashleigh decided they'd done enough for one day. She reined Lightning toward the fence and halted in front of the others.

"Oh, Ash, you did great!" Mona cried.

"Congratulations!" her mother called. "I can't believe how far the two of you have come."

"You look wonderful, Ashleigh," Mr. Griffen agreed.

Ashleigh patted Lightning's neck. "We couldn't have done it without Kurt's help."

"Well, he's certainly shown he's a great teacher," said Mr. Griffen. "You're a man of many talents, Kurt!" Kurt was a quiet, reserved man, but he was grinning happily.

Ashleigh dismounted and pulled up the stirrup irons. She wrapped her arms around Lightning's neck. "And I've got a great big treat for you, girl! Carrots and apples. How does that sound?"

But in the back of Ashleigh's mind was the thought, *We've come this far, but how much longer will we be able to stay together? I don't want them to take you away from me, girl.*

7

"I don't know why they're waiting so long to let us know," Ashleigh fretted to Mona, stuffing her winter parka into her school locker. "Tomorrow is Thanksgiving and we still haven't heard anything. I thought they would have told us something by now."

"Maybe they're just not telling you because it's so obvious—you know they couldn't find a better home for her," Mona said. "She's a completely different horse than when we first saw her. She looks so good now— she's fattened up, her coat's shiny. Remember what a mess she was when we found her? And you look great on her, too, Ash—like you two were meant to be a team."

Ashleigh smiled. "You know, I do feel like me and Lightning are a team. Sometimes I think she reads my mind and does what I want before I've even asked. And when I go and talk to her in her stall about stuff, she acts like she understands."

Mona laughed. "Yeah, I kind of feel that way about Silver. I may be outgrowing her, but she still knows what I'm thinking. Still, I hope I really will get a horse at Christmastime. I'll always love Silver, but I need a full-sized horse. I wonder what it will be like. . . ." Mona mused.

"Have your parents dropped any more hints?" Ashleigh asked.

"My father's fixing up one of the empty stalls in the barn," Mona said, eyes twinkling. "When I asked him why, he said it was a project he's been meaning to do for a long time."

"So you think it's for your new horse?"

"Yup. Don't worry, Ash. It's going to work out for both of us. I can tell," Mona added, dreamily. "Picture it: you on Lightning, and me on . . . let me think . . . what should I name my new horse? I thought of a name last night. Oh, I know—Frisky. I was reading about that Thoroughbred, Frisky Mister, who won sixteen races straight in Puerto Rico and over here. Then he ran badly in the Triple Crown when he came down with a virus that almost killed him. No one ever gave him much credit, because he didn't have a royal bloodline, but one of his foals sold at the Keeneland auction for pretty big bucks, remember?"

"Yeah, I remember," Ashleigh said. "I read in the

Daily Racing Form that his colts and fillies have been winning some big races. I like that name, Frisky. Frisky and Lightning," Ashleigh mused.

Both girls giggled, but they were dead serious about their dreams.

After school, Ashleigh brought Lightning out to ride on her own. They were comfortable with each other now, and Ashleigh felt safe as long as they stayed in the paddock.

Edgardale looked beautiful at that time of day. The sun was already low in the sky and there was a real nip to the air, but the sky was a still a vivid blue. The broodmares, foals, and yearlings were out in their paddocks, all bundled up in colorful turnout rugs, grazing quietly before they were brought in for their evening grain.

Today, Ashleigh wanted to work on her walk-to-canter transitions. After warming Lightning up at a walk and trot, Ashleigh moved her outside leg just behind the girth and urged the mare into a smooth canter. Lightning cantered on, leading with the inside leg so she'd be more balanced in the circle. Ashleigh followed the movement of the canter with her seat. When a rider was settled in the saddle properly and in control, the gait could feel very much like being on a rocking horse—the canter was much less bouncy than the trot and easier to ride. Ashleigh was trying to achieve that rocking-horse feeling now.

Silently, Ashleigh thanked Moe for all he'd taught her. Of course, she was learning even more now with Kurt's instruction. But Moe had always been there for Ashleigh to experiment with—trying out everything she had heard, seen, or read about riding.

Ashleigh brought Lightning down to a walk, and walked on until she reached the end of the paddock. Then, as she put her outside leg back behind the girth again, Lightning sprung into a canter. This time, she felt uneven. Ashleigh glanced down and saw that the mare was leading with her outside leg. She immediately checked her, easing her down to a sitting trot, and then asked for the canter once more. This time Lightning led off correctly, with the inside leg. They circled the entire paddock once, and then Ashleigh reined Lightning through a series of smaller circles, and wide figure eights. She would rein back at the narrow part of the figure eight, and ask Lightning to change leads through the walk, before cantering in the opposite direction.

Ashleigh was elated. Lightning was going so well. They were totally in sync and learning fast—together.

Ashleigh had always loved to ride, but she had never felt the thrill of actually teaching a horse something. Maybe Lightning had been ridden before, but if Ashleigh hadn't taken it slowly and gained Lightning's trust, they would never have been cantering around in such a relaxed way like they were today. All her efforts had really paid off.

Then, suddenly, Lightning's head went up and she snorted. Her canter faltered and her ears pricked in alarm. Ashleigh tried to get Lightning's attention back. She clucked and squeezed her calves to remind Lightning that she was still up there on her back, but instead of continuing at an easy canter, Lightning bolted in panic. Ashleigh was caught completely by surprise.

She tried to remember all she'd been taught to do in a situation like this. If a horse seems out of control, sit back in the saddle, hold the reins steady and firm, and most importantly: Keep your head. Don't panic or lean forward. The horse will only take that as a signal to go faster.

Ashleigh's mind was a blur as Lightning galloped madly across the paddock. Lightning didn't respond to Ashleigh's deep seat or her pressure on the reins. She charged on toward the fence at the far end of the paddock. For several terrifying moments, Ashleigh thought Lightning was actually going to jump the fence.

Then she remembered another lesson her parents had taught her. The easiest way to get control of a horse was to rein into a circle. Ashleigh tightened her left rein, drawing Lightning's head in that direction. She applied pressure with her inside leg to give Lightning something to bend around, and kept her weight back in the saddle. Lightning continued to gallop, but now she was galloping away from the fence. Ashleigh held her in a tight circling motion, and gradually she dropped down into a canter, then a trot, and finally a walk. Lightning snorted nervously.

"It's okay, girl," Ashleigh soothed, taking the opportunity to breathe. "I don't know what frightened you, but it's okay now. Let's just take it easy."

Lightning's ears flicked back as she listened to Ashleigh's words. Ashleigh kept the mare at a walk and continued in a wide circle. Ashleigh could feel Lightning relaxing, and breathed out a sigh of relief.

Then Ashleigh heard a strange sound herself. Now that she had Lightning under control again, she glanced back toward the barn to see a group of people striding over the grass in their direction. One of them was wearing a red coat and he carried an umbrella that he waved in the air every time he laughed his loud laugh. Another had two yipping terriers on leashes that barked at Lightning from under the paddock fence. Ashleigh was too busy keeping Lightning calm to get a good look, but now she understood what had spooked Lightning. The mare's acute hearing had picked up on the loud voices long before Ashleigh had.

What are these people doing here? Ashleigh wondered. She didn't recognize their car, and Edgardale rarely had visitors. And why were they being so noisy? Was it someone from the humane society again?

Lightning wasn't used to loud crowds, and Ashleigh kept her circling at the far end of the paddock, as far away from the observers as she could get. She saw that her parents and Kurt had joined the group, but not before they'd lined up along the paddock fence and were staring and gesturing in their direction. Ashleigh's father herded the crowd away from the paddock and into the barn. Ashleigh could imagine him trying to be charming, offering to show them the rest of the Edgardale grounds. She waited until they had retreated before she dared walk Lightning toward the bottom of the paddock and out the gate.

As she walked Lightning toward the barn, she was relieved to see Kurt approaching. He soothed Lightning with his voice, "Okay, Lightning. You're going to be fine. They're all gone. That's it. Easy, girl." When he got close enough, he patted Lightning's neck, looking up at Ashleigh.

"I saw what happened," he said. "Are you all right?"

Ashleigh nodded.

Kurt gripped Lightning's reins just below her muzzle. "Well, you did great," he said to Ashleigh. "Considering the circumstances, it could have been a lot worse."

"Who were those people anyway?" Ashleigh asked.

"The Friends of the Humane Society," Kurt answered. "The humane society benefactors. And they obviously don't have a clue about horses."

Ashleigh slid out of Lightning's saddle. Her legs felt weak beneath her as she landed. "Mom and Dad didn't say anything about them coming."

"That's because your parents didn't know. Neither did I."

Ashleigh frowned. "That's pretty rude, showing up here without telling us they were coming. My parents must be mad."

"Well, I wouldn't blame them if they are, but I think they tried their best to be polite."

Ashleigh was angry herself. Lightning didn't need this sort of disturbance, especially not with Ashleigh on her back. It could take days for her to go back to completely trusting Ashleigh when she rode her again. They may have undone what she had worked so hard to accomplish. She knew her parents were happy to give tours of the farm, but they always warned any visitors not to do anything that might spook the horses. These people just barged in and did as they pleased.

"So, I guess they came to see Lightning," she said grimly. "I hope they enjoyed the good part, when she was running away with me across the paddock."

"I don't think they meant any harm," Kurt said, patting Ashleigh's shoulder. "They're the people who give or raise money to support the humane society. Without their help, very few animals could be saved. They just don't know much about the animals they are trying to save. You see, they never actually work with the animals themselves."

Ashleigh was still angry that they'd showed up at Edgardale, but even more, she was scared about what their visit could mean for her and Lightning.

Kurt held open the paddock gate and Ashleigh led Lightning out and down to the barn. Ashleigh quickly brought the mare into her stall and untacked her. Through the open barn door, she saw the Friends of the Humane Society group still gathered out on the drive where her parents were talking to them.

Ashleigh ignored them and set to work brushing Lightning's white coat vigorously to relax both herself and the mare. Lightning munched her hay, happy to be back in her stall.

"So this is our horse!" a voice suddenly boomed outside the stall, startling Ashleigh. She looked up to see the man with the umbrella and the woman who'd been holding the dogs standing outside, looking into the stall. "She looked good working in the paddock—the little we got to see."

Ashleigh felt a chill go down her spine and felt a surge of anger, too. They hadn't even bothered to introduce themselves.

"Can you bring her out so we can get a better look at her?" the man demanded in a loud voice, although it sounded like more of an order than a request.

He turned to the woman, who must have put her dogs in the car. "You've seen the photos of her when she was rescued, haven't you? We're planning on using the before and after shots in our fund-raising campaign this year. I think it will be a terrific way to show what the society can do to rehabilitate an abused animal."

Ashleigh fumed silently. *What the* society *can do?* she thought. *They haven't done anything except leave Lightning in our loving care. They didn't even rescue her.* Ashleigh wasn't about to be bossed around in her own home by these people who knew nothing about horses.

"No, I'm sorry I can't bring her out," Ashleigh told them as politely as her anger allowed. "She's eating. Besides, she's had a rough day and needs to rest. Maybe some other time."

The man looked at Ashleigh and frowned. "What do you mean, you won't bring her out?" he said gruffly. "She's the property of the humane society, and I'm the head of its fund-raising committee. I'd like to have a better look at her."

"Sorry," Ashleigh said. "She was really upset when you all crowded around before and I think she's had enough for one day."

"I can't see how bringing her out of her stall is going to upset her," the woman cut in. "I'm sure the owner of the farm would agree. And anyway, aren't you awfully young to be working as a groom? Can we speak to your manager?"

Ashleigh bristled. "I'm the owner's daughter," she said through gritted teeth. "I'm the one who found Lightning. I brought her food and helped rescue her. I've taken care of her almost all by myself because my parents knew I'd do a good job. I really care about her—a lot. The humane society hasn't done anything except come here and look at her once in a while." As soon as the words were out of her mouth, Ashleigh regretted them. She knew she'd made these people angry, and that would do nothing to encourage the society to let the Griffens adopt Lightning. *Oh, no. I blew it,* she thought. *Why couldn't I just keep my mouth shut?*

The woman's face reddened, and the man glared at Ashleigh, tapping his umbrella on the barn floor. "That doesn't give you the right to insult me, young lady," the woman fumed. "I wonder what your parents will have to say about your lack of manners. And if you ask me, you didn't look like you could control the horse when you were riding her!" She turned on her heel and stalked away, the man following close behind her.

Ashleigh buried her face in Lightning's neck. "Oh, girl. Why couldn't I keep my big mouth shut? I made those people so angry, and now they won't want to let me keep you." Lightning blew out a few soft breaths. Ashleigh looked up into her eyes. "But I just had to stand up to them, didn't I?" she wailed.

Lightning huffed. She certainly didn't understand everything Ashleigh was saying, but she sensed the emotion behind her words. Ashleigh resumed her grooming, running a soft-bristled brush over Lightning's thick, white coat, letting her anger and worry subside.

A moment later, Ashleigh's parents came to the stall door. *Okay, this is it,* Ashleigh thought. *I'm in serious trouble.*

Instead, she was surprised. "Ash," Mrs. Griffen said, "I'm proud of you for standing up to those people."

Ashleigh spun around and stared at her mother in surprise. "You are?"

"Yes. They had no reason to come in here and tell you what to do with a horse under our care. I told them as much. I also told all of them how much you've done, all by yourself, to bring this mare back from near starvation and abuse. Your father and I made it clear to them that you've devoted hours and hours to caring for Lightning, rehabilitating and training her, and that you deserved the credit for her fantastic appearance and good health now."

"What did they say?" Ashleigh asked.

"Not a lot," her father said. "People like that are devoted to raising and giving money to good causes—and that's an honorable thing—but they sometimes can't see the forest for the trees."

"I've probably ruined our chances of adopting Lightning," Ashleigh said.

"We don't know that," her mother said honestly. "You

certainly got the fund-raisers worked up. But they can't argue with the good care we've given Lightning."

Ashleigh suddenly felt hot tears welling behind her eyelids, and looked down. "But they could still take Lightning. And I couldn't stand it—she needs me, and I need her!"

"Ashleigh," her father said, "if it's any consolation, if they don't agree to our adopting Lightning, your mother and I will fight tooth and nail to make sure she goes to an equally good home."

Ashleigh felt the tears streaking down her cheeks. She appreciated what her parents said, but her heart was heavy. She had known it was a possibility, but she couldn't imagine actually losing Lightning after all they'd been through together, and with all the dreams she had for their future.

"Ashleigh, we don't know what will happen yet," her mother said. "We just wanted to prepare you for every outcome. No one has made any decisions about Lightning, and I think that the facts still rule in your favor. How could anyone on that committee say that you hadn't done a fantastic job with Lightning, or that you don't deserve to keep her?"

Ashleigh nodded and swiped a hand across her cheeks to wipe the tears away. She knew what her mother said was true, but she wasn't reassured.

8

"How about some early Christmas shopping after school?" Mrs. Griffen asked Ashleigh brightly over breakfast. It was a half-day at school, as the following day was Thanksgiving—a holiday Ashleigh usually loved, because it was the beginning of the Christmas season. But this year Ashleigh couldn't work up any enthusiasm at all.

Ashleigh's first thought was that her mother was offering to take the wrong daughter shopping. Ashleigh hated shopping, but Caroline would have jumped at her mother's offer. Still, Ashleigh agreed to go—anything to distract her from worrying about Lightning. Instead of taking the bus home, her mother picked her up after school, and they headed into town to the local shops.

"I know you hate the mall," Mrs. Griffen said as she drove, "and it doesn't have a decent tack store, does it?"

Ashleigh knew how hard her mother was working to cheer her up, but that only made Ashleigh more depressed. Her mother wouldn't be doing this if she didn't think that Ashleigh would soon be getting bad news about Lightning.

The town had already been decorated for the holidays, with fake snow drifts, pine boughs, red bows, and Santa Clauses in the store windows. In Hiram's Saddlery, they chatted to other breeders and horse people they saw only when they went into town or at races. Ashleigh stopped to admire a saddle tied with a red satin ribbon in the window. She couldn't help thinking how perfect the saddle would be for Lightning. She breathed in the scent of leather and moved on to gape at the store's displays of beautiful riding clothes and tack, grooming equipment and horse blankets, trinkets and books—everything for the horse and horse owner, and all of it very expensive.

Ashleigh had been saving her allowance money for Christmas presents. She picked out a T-shirt with a funny horse cartoon on the back for her father, and a Breyer model pony that looked like Moe for Rory. She knew she'd never find anything for Caroline in here, but she couldn't resist buying a small plaque engraved with Lightning's name to attach to her halter.

Ashleigh noticed her mother was spending a lot of

time in the saddlery section, and she took the opportunity to pick out a pair of horseshoe earrings to give her. Ashleigh paid the cashier, tucked the bag under her arm and went to find her mother.

"Had enough?" her mother asked.

Ashleigh nodded. "I think I've found most of my presents. Shopping is okay, but it isn't that much fun when you don't have a lot of money to spend."

"I couldn't agree more," Mrs. Griffen said. "Too bad your sister doesn't think the same way."

When they got outside Ashleigh was surprised to see her father waiting by the car. Perhaps her mother had decided that buying Ashleigh that saddle was too big a decision to make alone, and she'd called her father for his opinion. Wishful thinking.

"Hi, Dad," Ashleigh said cheerfully. "What're you doing here?"

"Well, it's a secret," Mr. Griffen said.

"A secret?" Ashleigh asked, curious now. Whatever it was, it sounded exciting.

"We have something we want to show you," Mrs. Griffen answered mysteriously.

They all got into the car and headed down the main street out of town. Ashleigh was smiling and full of expectation as they drove along. Then they slowed down and pulled into a long driveway.

The sign in front said HOPEWELL CENTER. The drive was lined with old trees, and at its end was a large house, built of stone and covered in ivy. There was something very welcoming about the house and grounds. The drive continued past the house to a parking lot behind.

Now Ashleigh saw two immaculate white barns, with white-fenced paddocks extending beyond them toward the wooded hills behind. There were kids her own age running around in the playground behind the main house.

The Griffens got out of the van. "What is this place?" Ashleigh asked. "Is it a horse farm? What are all these kids doing here?"

"This is a child cancer research and rehabilitation center," her mother said, taking Ashleigh's arm.

"Cancer?" Ashleigh immediately thought of Kurt's daughter who had died of leukemia. She looked again at the children. Now she noticed that some of them were terribly thin; others had lost their hair. Ashleigh felt a knot in her stomach knowing all of them were so ill. "But what are we doing here? I don't understand."

"Ashleigh," Mrs. Griffen said, "I know this is going to be hard for you, but we're here because the humane society has recommended this center as a possible new home for Lightning."

Her mother's words took Ashleigh's breath away. She stared in shock, hoping she'd misunderstood. "Lightning . . . here?" Her mother nodded. "But . . . but . . . I thought you wanted us to adopt her. How can you let them take her away from me now?" Ashleigh's throat was so tight, she felt like she was choking. Tears welled in her eyes. "No . . . please, don't."

"We did plan on adopting Lightning, Ashleigh," Mr. Griffen said gently, "but this center also approached the humane society about adopting her after all the publicity over her rescue. One of the women who works with the children is an experienced horsewoman who uses riding as part of her rehabilitation techniques. Hopewell has lots of animals, but no horses, which is why they're interested in Lightning. The humane society suggested we come over and take a look at the facilities before any final decisions were made."

Ashleigh felt like she'd been punched in the stomach. She couldn't take it in. Give Lightning up after all they'd been through together? What about all the plans and dreams she'd had for them? Didn't any of it matter?

"Ash," Mrs. Griffen said gently, "remember, nothing's been decided. Let's just take a look around and talk to the people here."

Ashleigh numbly followed her parents to the rear entrance where they were greeted by a smiling, dark-haired woman who introduced herself as Marge Conti. "Welcome to Hopewell," she said, shaking the Griffens' hands. "I'm the director and I'm so pleased you could come."

"This is our daughter, Ashleigh," Mrs. Griffen said. "She found Lightning, and has been caring for her."

"It's so nice to finally meet you, Ashleigh," the director said sincerely. "We all fell in love with Lightning when we saw that newspaper article right after she was rescued. She looked so pathetic, and our patients here just couldn't understand how anyone could treat her so badly. The patients have sort of become a Lightning fan club and the humane society has kept us up to date about her progress while she's been at Edgardale. From all I've heard you've done a wonderful job in rehabilitating her, and we're eager to give Lightning a new and loving home here."

Ms. Conti turned back to Ashleigh's parents before she could see Ashleigh wince.

A new home for Lightning? Ashleigh was stunned. It was as if she was being pulled under water and was far too disoriented to swim to the surface. *The humane society had been giving these people updates on Lightning? Had they known all along that Lightning* would come here? Had they let Ashleigh become attached to the horse she'd helped save, without ever bothering to tell Ashleigh and her family that they had no hope of adopting Lightning? How could the humane society be so cruel? Ashleigh wondered. She'd always thought they did such good work—saving so many unwanted animals and finding them good homes— but she didn't understand them now. Why take Lightning away from a good home and from the very person who'd rescued her?

"Shall I give you a tour of our facilities? We try to use the most up-to-date methods in treating our patients and providing them with a comfortable, caring environment. Let me show you through the building first," Marge Conti continued, as she began to lead them down a long corridor.

Ashleigh was barely listening as Marge took them through the comfortably furnished rooms. The first was the communal living room. There was a ping-pong table, two TV sets, overstuffed chairs and couches scattered all around the room, shelves and tables stacked with books and games, and even a computer. A little blond boy about Rory's age was quietly reading in a wheelchair near one of the tall windows. Suddenly, Ashleigh felt a pang of guilt for dwelling on her own sadness.

On the other side of a main hall and staircase was the dining room, but instead of one long table, smaller tables had been placed around the room, almost like a restaurant, each with four to six chairs and colorful place mats.

"The kitchen and offices are through there," Ms. Conti motioned to a door at the rear of the room, "and through here is our treatment wing." She led them through a second door and down a carpeted corridor with rooms to either side.

The wing had the antiseptic smell of a hospital, but aside from the medical equipment, it didn't look like any hospital Ashleigh had ever been in. She still had horrible memories of her brief stay in one when she was six and had her tonsils removed. Here there was color everywhere, posters on the walls, and pretty curtains in the windows. Several nurses—men and women dressed in cheery blue and yellow uniforms—rushed around, smiling pleasantly at the Griffens as they walked by.

"At the end of this wing is our swimming pool and whirlpool baths. Patients find the water soothing after treatments," Marge Conti explained. "Upstairs are all the patients' bedrooms, which they're allowed to decorate themselves."

They continued their tour outside and went into

one of the barns, where there were a number of stalls. Everything was neat and had the clean smell of hay. Despite herself, Ashleigh was filled with delight as Ms. Conti introduced the barn's occupants, all adopted from animal rescue organizations. There was Barney, the black-and-white goat; Olie, the pot-bellied pig; half a dozen cats who lounged on the stall partitions; two chickens, Daisy and Pumpkin; and Mortimer the duck, who lorded it over them all, standing guard and quacking loudly as they toured the barn. A number of children were cleaning, feeding, and playing with Olie the pig, Barney the goat, and the chickens.

It was a nice place, Ashleigh had to admit, as Mortimer the duck waddled behind her and her parents, quacking a warning to the intruders.

Another woman led several children into the barn. "Ah, here's our horse person," Marge Conti said with a smile. "Sally, come over and meet the Griffens, and tell them something about what you do."

Sally was about Ashleigh's mother's age, tall and lean in jeans and sweatshirt. "Always nice to meet fellow horse people," she said. "I understand you run a breeding farm."

"We do. Edgardale, on the other side of town," Mr. Griffen acknowledged. "We're still a fairly small operation, but growing."

"And you must be Ashleigh, the rescue girl," she said to Ashleigh.

"Yes, that's me," Ashleigh said reluctantly. She had been trying to find fault with Hopewell, looking for a reason why it wouldn't make a good home for Lightning. But Ashleigh couldn't help herself from immediately taking to Sally—it was hard not to, she was so friendly.

"How's Lightning coming along?" Sally asked. "We all saw those pictures of her in the paper right after she was rescued. She was a pretty sorry sight."

"She's doing great," Ashleigh said, responding to the woman's genuine interest and forgetting for the moment that she could be losing Lightning to Sally. "She's put on a lot of weight. Her coat's really shining now. And I've been riding her, too."

"Good for you," Sally exclaimed. "That's a lot of work for someone your age. How old are you? About eleven?"

"Ten," Ashleigh said.

"You know there's someone here I'd like you to meet. Her name is Kira, she's your age, and she loves horses, too. Why don't you come with me, and I'll introduce you."

Ashleigh followed Sally back down the barn aisle to a group of kids who were playing with the animals. Sally paused by one of the stalls and called, "Kira, could you come here a minute? I'd like you to meet Ashleigh, the girl who rescued that poor white horse."

Kira came out of the stall and looked curiously at Ashleigh, then smiled. She had dark brown hair, like Ashleigh, but hers was only about an inch long. "I've been reading about Lightning in the paper," Kira said excitedly, "only they didn't say much about the girl who rescued her. Wow, that must have been exciting!"

"Well, it was pretty scary, too. The man who owned her was so mean. My friend and I were terrified he'd catch us feeding her."

"I just want to show your parents something," Sally said, leaving the two girls alone.

"Oh, before you ask about my hair," Kira said casually, rubbing a hand over her short-cropped hair. "It's my chemotherapy. It helps, but sometimes it makes your hair fall out."

"But it's growing back," Ashleigh said, trying to look on the bright side.

"Yeah, unless I have to have chemo again. But I'm doing okay right now," Kira said. Then she swiftly changed the subject. "You know, before I got sick, I was taking riding lessons. I loved it. I was learning to jump. I wish I could still ride," she said with a shrug, "but there aren't any horses here."

Ashleigh had never met anyone with cancer before. She had expected Kira to act differently—more weak and sickly. Ashleigh was pleasantly surprised. Kira was a normal kid who loved horses, just like her.

"My friend, Mona, really likes jumping, too. She's been training her pony, Silver. I'm more interested in racing. I love to gallop. And my family has a Thoroughbred breeding farm," Ashleigh gushed.

"Wow. You are so lucky. I'd love to live on a horse farm," Kira said dreamily. "I love animals, but horses are the greatest. But I guess you know that."

Ashleigh grinned. "Yeah, they really are. You know I've been training Lightning and I started riding her a few weeks ago. She was in really bad shape at first, but now we go out almost every day."

"You must ride a lot," Kira said.

"Whenever I can. Before I found Lightning, I rode our pony, Moe, but I'm really outgrowing him. My younger brother rides him now."

"Sally's hoping the center can get a pony or horse, but she hasn't found one yet. If she does, I'm definitely going to be the first to ride!" Kira's smile lit up her pale face.

Then it dawned on Ashleigh: *Kira didn't know the*

center was trying to adopt Lightning. What should I say? Ashleigh wondered.

"Have you been here long?" Ashleigh asked, suddenly feeling a little uncomfortable.

"About six months. I was really sick at first, but lately I've been going home for weekends. We live in Ohio, but my parents said this center was the best around. At least I've made it through six months here. Some kids don't even make it that long."

Ashleigh understood the meaning behind Kira's words—some kids died.

"But my doctor, who's a really neat lady, says that if everything goes okay for the next month, I may be able to go home," Kira added brightly, although Ashleigh couldn't understand how anyone could be so cheerful in Kira's situation.

Ashleigh's parents returned with Sally.

"It looks like you two are getting along," Sally said. "You've been talking a mile a minute."

Ashleigh laughed. "Well, we're both into horses. Oh, Mom and Dad, this is Kira."

"Nice to meet you, Kira," Ashleigh's mother said. "Sally tells us you've been helping her out a lot with the animals."

"It's fun," Kira said, "and last week I went with her to her handicapped-riders class."

"She was telling us all about it," Mrs. Griffen said, "and how much riding helps with balance and self-confidence, too."

"She's going to take me again this week, aren't you, Sally?"

"As long as you're up to it."

"Well, Ashleigh," Mr. Griffen said, "I hate to interrupt your talk, but we have to go. The horses must be wondering if they're going to get fed tonight. I hope we'll see you again, Kira."

"Me too," Kira said. "Will you come visit again, Ashleigh?" she asked.

Ashleigh felt torn in a dozen different pieces. She really liked Kira, but she couldn't bear the thought of losing Lightning. It was strange, too, that Kira didn't know why Ashleigh and her parents had come there. Ashleigh had never felt so awkward.

"I've got an idea. Maybe Sally could bring you and some of the other kids over to our farm for a tour," Mrs. Griffen suggested, glancing at Sally for approval.

Kira's eyes instantly brightened. "Oh, can we Sally? Please!"

"Since we've been officially invited," Sally answered with a fond smile, "I'll see what I can do."

"Yes!" Kira beamed. "I'm so glad I got to meet you, Ashleigh."

"I'm glad I met you, too." Ashleigh smiled weakly. She just wished they'd met under different circumstances, and that Lightning's future wasn't involved.

9

"Ashleigh," her mother said from the front seat. "I understand what you're going through right now, and it's a big decision to have on your shoulders—too big maybe. But please remember that you don't have to give Lightning away. You saved that mare's life. The humane society felt that the children here would really benefit from having Lightning, especially since Sally is an experienced horse person, but I don't think they would ever force you to give her up."

"They'd have a real public relations fiasco if they did," Mr. Griffen put in. "And I'd be the first one out there protesting."

It was nice to know that Ashleigh had her parents' support, but at the moment it was little comfort. By the time the Griffens' car had reached the end of Hopewell's drive, Ashleigh was feeling torn apart and confused. She would have liked so much to help the kids at Hopewell and make their lives happier. But for months she'd thought of Lightning as her own horse—or, at least, that she would eventually be her own horse. Ashleigh had made so many plans for what they would do together, and those plans had seemed truly possible . . . until now. She thought of Lightning and how much she would miss the mare. She felt like her heart was breaking.

Ashleigh's mother continued. "The humane society just wanted us to let you see another home where Lightning could go and be given equal love. I suppose they figure that because you live on a horse farm, you have no real need for Lightning. They just don't realize how attached to her you've become."

"But I helped rescue her. I've taken care of her and made her healthy and fit and beautiful again. They wouldn't want her if she still looked like she did when Mona and I found her!" Ashleigh was so close to tears, she had to blink her eyes to keep them back. "It's not fair. I love Lightning, and she loves me. Why can't they find another horse?"

"Ashleigh," her father said, "no one is trying to tell you what to do. If you want to keep the mare that much, we'll tell the humane society that we definitely want to keep her. I know it's an awful burden to put on your shoulders, but we'll be behind you whatever you decide."

"But then I keep thinking about those poor kids," Ashleigh said. "They're all sick, and some of them might even die, like Kurt's daughter."

Both of Ashleigh's parents were silent for a moment. Then her mother said, "We can discuss this over Thanksgiving. We all have a lot to think about."

Ashleigh was silent the rest of the way home. The air in the car was thick with tension. Ashleigh knew her parents were thinking about Kurt and his daughter, but Ashleigh's mind was heavy with indecision. *What is the right thing to do? And what will be best for Lightning?*

It was dark when they arrived home. Ashleigh jumped out of the van and ran straight to Lightning's stall. She knew Kurt would have brought the horses in for the night, even though he was working alone. Sure enough, Lightning was in her stall looking alert, the picture of health. Her body was well-muscled, her white coat shining. Ashleigh went into the tack box outside her stall and took out a couple of carrots before letting herself inside.

Lightning welcomed her with a gleeful whinny, especially when she saw the treats Ashleigh held in her hand. She knew she spoiled Lightning with too many treats to make up for the harsh treatment the mare had endured before, but they were all healthy treats, like carrots and apples. She only sneaked in an occasional sugar cube.

"It hasn't been a very good day today," Ashleigh said to the mare as Lightning chomped on a carrot. "I just don't know what to do, girl. I really might lose you. It's my decision, but I just feel like crying, because I don't want to give you up. Oh, Lightning!" She threw her arms around the mare's neck. "I love you so much!"

Lightning didn't understand all of Ashleigh's words, but she sensed Ashleigh's sadness. Whickering, she touched Ashleigh's shoulder with her nose as if to comfort her.

Kurt walked up to the stall and looked in over the half door. "Uh-oh," he said, seeing Ashleigh's tears.

"I'm sorry," Ashleigh said miserably.

Kurt sighed and pushed his hair back off his forehead. "I know that the humane society has been thinking about donating Lightning to Hopewell. I'm sorry I didn't tell you before, but I wasn't sure they'd follow through." He hesitated nervously. "You see, I've been working with the kids at Hopewell myself. After my daughter's death, I felt like I had to do something. I knew they'd approached the humane society after seeing the write-up about Lightning's rescue in the papers. But I knew how much you loved her, and how heartbroken you'd be if she was taken away from you—which it sounded like they had decided to do. I objected to their decision, and so did Marge and Sally at Hopewell. We felt you should have some say. It's your decision, Ashleigh, and I know how hard it is."

"So you think I should keep her?" Ashleigh asked, searching for an easy answer.

"Well," Kurt said. "You deserve to keep her. Hopewell would give her a wonderful home, too, but I feel like the Friends of the Humane Society have a selfish motive for donating her to Hopewell. Letting a children's cancer center adopt Lightning would bring them a lot more publicity than leaving her with you."

"Then why do I even have to think about giving her up?" Ashleigh cried. But she knew why: Kira, and the other kids at the center. Ashleigh shivered, but it wasn't from the cold evening air.

Kurt put a reassuring hand on her shoulder. "I can't tell you what to do. You're too young, I think, to have been asked to make this kind of decision, but I'll support you, whatever you decide. And I'm here if you need any advice."

Ashleigh got Lightning settled and went up to the house for dinner. It was a somber meal. Everyone pointedly avoided the subject of Lightning. Ashleigh barely touched her food, but her parents didn't scold her. Everyone was treating her like she was made of glass. After dinner, she ran upstairs to call Mona.

"Oh, Mona, it's been such a bad, bad day," Ashleigh wailed into the phone.

"What happened?" Mona asked in alarm.

Ashleigh explained everything, pouring her heart out and bursting into tears once more.

"No, but that's not fair," Mona cried, outraged. "How could they ask you to give Lightning away after all you've done for her? I don't believe it!"

"I don't *have* to give her to Hopewell," Ashleigh weighed the thought in her head as she spoke. "They said the decision is up to me, but, Mona, those poor sick kids. A lot of them are really little, but there were some our age, too. I met this girl, Kira, who used to ride before she got sick. I liked her a lot, and I keep thinking about how having Lightning there would make her so happy. She loves horses, and she loves to jump. She's been going through chemotherapy, and her hair is only just growing back, but she's just a normal kid. I'm sure she would love Lightning. They don't have any horses there at all." Ashleigh felt like crying again. "Oh, Mona, I don't know what to do!"

"Do you have to decide right away?" Mona asked.

"Well, not this minute, but soon. Oh—would it be selfish if I decided to keep her?"

"Of course not, Ashleigh! If it hadn't been for you, she'd probably be dead by now, the way that awful man treated her."

"You helped, too."

"But you nursed her back to health. The humane society wouldn't have Lightning to give away in the first place if you hadn't worked so hard to help her."

"I know," Ashleigh agreed. "But every time I think that, I see the faces of these kids at the center. A lot of them are going to die, Mona."

"Yeah, I know," Mona said somberly. "But it still wasn't fair to ask you to give up Lightning. There are other horses that the center could adopt."

When Ashleigh hung up a few minutes later, she wasn't sure she felt any better. Usually talking a problem over with Mona helped her sort things out. *Why am I feeling so guilty about wanting to keep the horse I helped to save?* Ashleigh asked herself. *Why should I feel guilty at all?* It didn't make sense. She covered her face with her hands and wished it would all go away.

On Thanksgiving morning, Ashleigh awoke early to a house already filled with good smells. She knew her mother had put the turkey in the oven so that it would be ready for their afternoon meal. The sun was shining in through her window and the last of the foliage glimmered in shades of gold and copper. It could have been the start of a great day, but all Ashleigh could think about was the dilemma facing her.

She got dressed quickly and went out to the barn to do her morning chores. They had a tradition at Edgardale to include the horses in the big holidays. At Thanksgiving, each of the horses had some special treats added to their feed buckets. Ashleigh went to the feed room and helped her mother measure grain and top off each bucket with apples, carrots, and a couple of peppermints. The horses loved the sweet taste of the mints.

When Ashleigh brought out Lightning's breakfast, the white mare snorted in excitement when she got a whiff of her feed pail. Ashleigh smiled. Lightning sure hadn't received any treats from her previous owner, but she seemed to be used to them now.

Since it was such a beautiful fall day, Mr. Griffen decided to buckle the horses into their blankets and put them all out in the paddocks. Ashleigh led Lightning out to her paddock and rested her arms on the top rail of the fence to watch her.

Lightning didn't need a blanket. The mixed-breed mare was growing a much thicker winter coat than the Thoroughbreds, and would just get hot moving around with a blanket on. That could make her sick in the chilly air.

Ashleigh thought of how much she would miss the sight of Lightning trotting across the paddock each morning and kicking up her heels before settling down to graze. Then she pushed the sad thought away and went back to the barn to work on her stalls.

Soon Caroline and Rory came out to join her. Rory went straight to Moe's stall and personally gave Moe his treats. Then he groomed the pony as Moe gobbled up the goodies. Since Lightning had arrived at Edgardale, Rory had taken a proprietary interest in the pony. Ashleigh was glad, because she no longer had as much time to spend with Moe.

The whole family chipped in to help with the preparations for the big dinner, except Rory, who camped out in front of the television to watch the Thanksgiving Day parades. Ashleigh and Caroline helped peel and cut up vegetables. Mr. Griffen lifted the heavy turkey from the oven for basting. Then he moved the kitchen table into the living room, as the farmhouse didn't have a formal dining room. The girls helped set the table, smoothed out their mother's best tablecloth, and took the china only used for special occasions from the cupboard.

"Don't forget the candles," Mrs. Griffen said, "and, Derek, can you get the drinks ready?"

For Thanksgiving and Christmas, Mr. Griffen mixed up a batch of Shirley Temples with lots of extra cherries for the kids, while the adults shared a special bottle of wine.

"What time did Kurt say he was coming over?" Mrs. Griffen asked her husband.

"I told him to come over before one o'clock. That way we'll have time to eat before Quest's race," Mr. Griffen said. Quest was scheduled to race again that afternoon at Belmont, her last race before she was shipped down to Gulfstream Park in Florida. They would all be watching. "Maybe Kurt and I can go over the breeding and foaling schedules I've put into the computer," Ashleigh's father went on.

"Oh, Derek, not on Thanksgiving!" Mrs. Griffen said.

Mr. Griffen winked at Ashleigh, who knew her dad just wanted to show off his new toy. Her parents had bought a computer for the business that spring, and her father was now hooked. "Kurt doesn't mind working on his day off," he said.

Kurt arrived a few minutes later. After Mr. Griffen

offered him a drink, they retreated into the study. Ashleigh, Caroline, and their mother sat down with Rory to watch the end of the Macy's Thanksgiving Day Parade. Ashleigh still loved the parade, but today she felt like she was just going through the motions of Thanksgiving. Her heart just wasn't in it.

"There's Santa!" Rory shouted, his face glowing, as Santa Claus arrived on his float at the parade's finale. "That means Christmas is almost here. I wish I could be there to tell Santa exactly what I want."

"There's still plenty of time to write to Santa at the North Pole and tell him what you want," Mrs. Griffen told him. "He reads all the letters he gets."

Rory turned to his mother. "Let's write my letter *now*."

"Let's wait until after we've had the turkey," Mrs. Griffen said. "Is everyone hungry?"

"Yes," Rory and Caroline called in unison. Ashleigh was silent. She hadn't felt hungry in days, although the Thanksgiving meal was usually her favorite.

Mrs. Griffen stuck her head into the study and called to Mr. Griffen and Kurt, who were both hunched over, staring at the computer screen. "I hate to bother you two, but it's time to eat."

While Mrs. Griffen, Caroline, and Ashleigh filled serving dishes with potatoes, vegetables, gravy, and stuffing, Mr. Griffen carved the turkey. Soon they were all seated at the table, filling their plates with mouthwatering food. Rory was fussy. "I only want turkey and potatoes," he insisted.

"You'll have some carrots, too, or I won't send that letter to Santa," Mrs. Griffen said. Everyone laughed as Rory began spooning carrots out of the serving dish and onto his plate.

Ashleigh took a long drink from her Shirley Temple and tried to muster up an appetite. She half listened to her parents and Kurt as they talked. Caroline looked totally bored. Rory rolled the carrots around on his plate. Ashleigh was just thinking about calling Mona to see if she wanted to watch Quest's race together, when her mother broke her train of thought.

"Oh! Derek, Ashleigh, Kurt—it completely slipped my mind," her mother exclaimed. "Sally from Hopewell called this morning while you were out in the barn. She wanted to know if it was all right to bring Kira and some of the other Hopewell children over to see the farm on Saturday. I was in the middle of cooking, but I told her yes. Does that sound all right?" she asked anxiously.

"That sounds fine with me, unless we get bad weather," Ashleigh's father said. "But then we could still give them a tour of the barn, and stay inside instead of going out in the paddocks."

Everyone looked at Ashleigh. She felt suddenly sick to her stomach. As much as she liked Kira and the other Hopewell kids, and as much as she wanted them all to enjoy their lives and get better, having them come to the farm to see Lightning for themselves scared her. She knew they would all fall instantly in love with her, and what then? Ashleigh knew she would feel guilty for even considering keeping Lightning. But in her heart of hearts, Ashleigh knew she really didn't want to let them have her. She wanted Lightning for herself.

Before Ashleigh could say anything, Caroline broke the silence. "You know, I was talking to one of my friends today, Ash," she said. "Her mother is on the fund-raising committee for the humane society. She says if you don't make your mind up about Lightning soon, they're going to come and take her."

Ashleigh let go of her fork and it clattered on her plate. She felt like the ground had suddenly dropped away and she was falling, out of control. She gripped the edge of her chair.

"Caroline!" Mrs. Griffen said sharply. "What you heard from your friend is rumor and gossip. You shouldn't be listening to it."

"It didn't sound like gossip to me, Mom," Caroline said.

Ashleigh stared at her sister. She knew Caroline wouldn't make up something like this just to hurt her. Caroline wasn't that mean.

"Enough, Caro!" Mr. Griffen said. "You're just trying to start trouble with your sister as usual."

"I am not!" Caroline protested. "I'm just telling her what I heard."

Ashleigh's face felt strange. She gripped her chair more tightly. She didn't want to cry and spoil everyone's dinner.

"Yes," Mr. Griffen said angrily, "but you heard it from people who don't care about what Ashleigh's done for Lightning; people who are very wealthy, and who support good causes, but have never had any real involvement with the animals they give money to protect. They are more interested in their image than in the animals."

Caroline ducked her head, but Ashleigh could see her sister didn't understand. Caroline was attracted to money and prestige, and tended to pick her friends that way. Ashleigh sat quietly while everyone continued talking and eating. She toyed with her food and mulled over Caroline's words. They were a sharp reminder that Ashleigh's dilemma wasn't going to go away.

Ashleigh's family and Kurt were all eating their pumpkin pie and watching the race at Edgardale, but Ashleigh had received special permission to go over to Mona's house. Mona's mother made hot cocoa with marshmallows, and the girls slurped it up as they watched the horses begin loading in the gate. The girls sat on the floor, eyes glued to Wanderer's Quest. Behind them, Mona's parents watched from the couch.

The jockeys circled their horses behind the gate while attendants loaded each horse in order of post position. Everything went smoothly until they tried to load Queenly Presence, the favorite, who had a reputation for being fractious. Ashleigh felt sorry for the horses and jockeys left standing in the gate while the attendants repeatedly tried to load the filly and failed. Thankfully Quest wasn't among those already loaded. Finally they blindfolded Queenly Presence, and with two attendants pulling at her head and two attendants pushing from behind with linked arms, they got her in. The rest of the field loaded quickly. Quest went in last. The gate doors had barely closed behind her when the starting bell sounded and the front gates flew open. Eight powerful and elegantThoroughbreds surged onto the track, vying for position.

Two fillies pulled ahead to set the pace. The favorite, who'd caused so much trouble earlier, raced just behind them in third. Quest settled in mid-pack, which was normal for her late running style.

Midway down the backstretch, Quest was still in mid-pack. "She looks like she's boxed in," Ashleigh said to Mona. "Get her off the rail!" Ashleigh muttered to the jockey, who, of course, couldn't hear her plea.

The horse outside of Quest began dropping back, leaving just enough room for Quest's jockey to shoot the filly through and angle her three wide as the field approached the far turn.

"Yes!" Mona cried. "Keep her going!"

The fractions for the first quarter and half had been brisk and had taken a toll on the front-runners. They started losing ground, and Queenly Presence shot past them and into the lead.

"And down the stretch they come!" the announcer cried. "It looks like the favorite is going to have her way today. She's opened up her lead to two lengths. . . ."

Ashleigh shut out the announcer's voice. She only had eyes for one horse. Quest was beginning to gain on the two fillies to her inside, but once she changed leads, she really began to roll. "Go!" Ashleigh screamed, pounding her fists on the floor. "Keep it up!"

It was thrilling to watch a horse that had been bred at Edgardale looking so good in a race. But Ashleigh wanted to race, too, someday. She longed to be in Quest's saddle, positioning the filly, urging her on, finding her best stride and using it to advantage.

"Come on!" Mona and her parents were cheering Quest on, too.

Quest continued gaining on the leader. But would she have enough ground to catch the other filly before the wire?

Quest was still running four wide down the stretch. Ashleigh hoped that Queenly Presence's jockey hadn't seen Quest coming. She held her breath. The wire was coming up so fast. Then Quest seemed to find yet another gear, and with two leaps, got her head in front, then her neck. They went under the wire—Quest the winner!

Ashleigh and Mona jumped to their feet and danced around in front of the TV. "She did it!" Ashleigh cried. "Oh, wow! I can hardly believe it!" She found herself hugging everyone in the room, including Mona's parents.

"It's good to see you smiling," Mona said. "You've been so down lately, worrying about Lightning."

"I know," Ashleigh agreed. "But I'm not going to let it get me down anymore," she said defiantly. She had meant to tell Mona what Caroline had said over Thanksgiving dinner, but the race had lifted her spirits, and Ashleigh didn't want to break the mood. "And I'm not going to give up either," she went on. "Lightning is mine if I decide to keep her," she said with new conviction, surprising even herself.

"That's right," Mona agreed.

"Anyway, I'd better head home before it gets dark. I'll bet my parents are celebrating big time. If it's nice tomorrow, do you want to bring Silver over and ride with me and Lightning on the lanes?"

"You're going to take Lightning out on the lanes?" Mona asked excitedly.

"Kurt thinks she's ready."

"I'll be there," Mona agreed.

Now that she had been riding Lightning, Ashleigh noticed how much the mare anticipated their daily workouts. As soon as Ashleigh approached the paddock where Lightning and Moe were grazing, the mare gave a loud whinny and came trotting toward the gate, as if she couldn't wait to go out for a ride.

Ashleigh had Lightning groomed and tacked up on

crossties by the time Mona trotted Silver down the drive. It was a cold morning and the girls were bundled up in parkas, scarves, and gloves. Soon the lanes would be a mess of frozen mud and their rides would be few and far between. Lightning stamped her feet impatiently as Ashleigh prepared to lead her out of the barn to mount up.

At first, Lightning seemed startled when, instead of leading her to the paddock, Ashleigh mounted up outside the barn and followed Mona and Silver up to the paddock lanes.

"Okay, girl. Let's just try and enjoy ourselves while we still can," Ashleigh murmured, to quiet her.

The two girls headed down the lanes, their horses stepping out brightly. Despite the colder weather, the grass was still green, although Ashleigh knew that wouldn't last for long.

Ashleigh was glad Mona and Silver were with them. Lightning seemed to relax and fall into step with Silver. But Ashleigh was quietly on her guard, in case anything sudden happened to set Lightning off.

Ashleigh couldn't stop smiling as she and Mona headed out. "I've been dreaming about doing this for so long," Ashleigh said, "and now I'm really doing it— riding Lightning out with you and Silver! Come on, let's trot," she said, urging Lightning forward.

"Except that I can't keep up with you anymore," Mona said good-naturedly. She and Silver had suddenly fallen behind. "Silver can't match Lightning's strides. She's two hands shorter, and her legs aren't as long as Lightning's."

"Yeah, but she gives it a good try," Ashleigh called. "And don't worry, we don't have to race. You'll be getting your horse soon. Then we can really have fun!" Then a shadow crossed Ashleigh's face. *If I still have Lightning,* she thought.

When Ashleigh and Mona returned from their ride, the sky had turned gray and it was getting even colder. They put the horses in the barn and went into the house to warm up and eat a late lunch of turkey sandwiches and hot chocolate. Then Mona had to go home and Ashleigh went down to the barn to see her and Silver off. Lightning was standing in her stall, dozing. Ashleigh could see Lightning's breath in the air, coming out of her velvety nostrils in big, slow puffs. *Maybe she* does *need a blanket for the winter,* Ashleigh thought. But before she could ask her parents to buy one, Ashleigh would have to decide Lightning's future.

10

Mona was doing her best to calm Ashleigh's nerves as they looked at horse magazines in Ashleigh's and Caroline's bedroom. Then Caroline came back from shopping with her friends. She frowned as she came into the room, dropping her bags on the floor and plopping down on her bed.

"Ash, I just talked to Mom. She told me those kids from the cancer center were coming over today," she said, rushing her words out. "I just wanted you to know that I'm really sorry about what I said at Thanksgiving dinner. I didn't mean—"

Ashleigh cut in. "It's okay, Caro. I would have wanted them to come and visit even if you hadn't said anything."

"Are you sure?" Caro asked worriedly.

Ashleigh nodded. *My sister can sometimes be totally self-centered,* Ashleigh thought, *but Caro's good side usually wins out in the end.*

Caroline still needed reassurance. "You're not mad at me, are you?"

"No, not anymore. I was on Thanksgiving, though," Ashleigh said, pulling on one of her riding boots. "Will you come out with us and meet the Hopewell kids when they come?"

"Maybe I will," Caroline answered thoughtfully.

The visitors from Hopewell Center were scheduled to arrive at three. It was a beautiful wintry Saturday, perfect for riding. Ashleigh had wanted her best friend to be there to meet Kira and the other kids from Hopewell, so Mona had come over in the morning, and they had taken Moe and Silver out for a gallop. Ashleigh was sure the Hopewell kids would want her to demonstrate on Lightning, so she waited to ride her until their visit. Ashleigh and Mona had spent the rest of the day helping to get the horses, paddocks, and barn in ship-shape for their visitors.

The whole of the Griffen family, Mona, and Kurt were waiting near the barn when the Hopewell van came down Edgardale's tree-lined drive. Ashleigh's stomach was suddenly filled with a thousand butterflies. She stamped her feet nervously and blew on her fingers, which were tingling with the cold.

Sally, smiling brightly, opened the driver's door and jumped out. "This is so wonderful of you," she said warmly to the Griffens. "I can't thank you enough for letting us tour your farm."

Sally opened the van's side door. "Okay, guys, here we are. I hope you remember to thank the Griffens for their hospitality."

Seven Hopewell patients tumbled out of the van. Each one showed some signs of their illness—gaunt and pale faces, thinned hair from chemotherapy—but their eyes were bright with expectation, and their cheeks were rosy. They were all bundled up in parkas to keep out the frosty air. Sally wheeled an eighth passenger in a wheelchair down the van's handicapped ramp—the little blond boy about Rory's age who Ashleigh recognized from her tour. Ashleigh spotted Kira at the back of the group, and the girls waved to each other. Ashleigh didn't want to interrupt her dad. She could talk to Kira when he was done with his tour.

"Hello, everyone," Mr. Griffen said to the children. "We're so glad to have you here. Edgardale is a small breeding farm, but if you like horses, we've sure got them."

Somebody giggled out loud. It was the boy in the wheelchair, who couldn't have been more than five.

He called out to Mr. Griffen. "I'm Kyle. I really would like to ride a Thoroughbred one day."

"There's no reason why you can't," Mr. Griffen called back. "But first maybe you should try a pony, which would be a little more your size."

Ashleigh watched her father lead the group on. Everyone at Edgardale had made the tour as easy as possible for the children by putting the horses in the paddocks closest to the barn, even making use of the pastures that were supposed to be rested until spring.

"Let's start by going to the paddocks," Mr. Griffen continued, "so you can see our weanlings. I know everyone loves baby horses, but they grow so fast. Our weanlings don't quite look like babies anymore. Most of them are well over six months old, and they've gotten pretty big."

Ashleigh saw that what her father said was true. The weanlings had grown into their long, spindly legs and muscled out. They no longer had the gangly looks of very young foals, but their antics at play were still funny to watch. They chased each other across the paddock, kicking up their heels and holding mock battles. Sometimes, in their enthusiasm, they stumbled to the ground, then quickly rose, shaking themselves, to charge off again. The children loved it, laughing at the weanlings' play and asking lots of questions.

"How old are they?"

"What's that one called?"

Ashleigh's father continued to charm the Hopewell kids with fun facts about the horses that they could understand and enjoy.

"All of these weanlings will officially become yearlings, or one-year old, on January first, even though most of them won't be a year old until several months later. That birth date was set by the rules of the Jockey Club. Since most races are restricted to particular age groups, it's much simpler to have all horses turn a year older on the same date. You guys wouldn't like it because you wouldn't have as many birthday parties to go to—just one *big* one."

It was a side of her father Ashleigh rarely saw, but she knew he had to make similar explanations to prospective buyers who often didn't know that much about horses themselves and depended on breeders and trainers to make the decisions for them. He was really hamming it up, and sounded like he was enjoying every minute of it.

As Ashleigh's father spoke, Ashleigh watched his young audience. Despite being sick, the Hopewell kids looked bright-eyed and excited as they watched the horses. Kira was absolutely enthralled.

"I want to ride that little black horse!" Kyle pointed to the coal black colt scampering around the paddock.

"That's Tonka," Mr. Griffen said. "You have a good eye for horses. He's only a baby now, but he's the best in our crop this year."

Kyle grinned and looked pleased with himself. Ashleigh hoped his wish would come true, and that he could someday ride a horse like Tonka.

Mona nudged Ashleigh's elbow and whispered in her ear. "They're so cute," she said, giggling at Kyle's enthusiasm. "It looks like they're really having fun."

"Yeah," Ashleigh agreed. "Come on, I want you to meet Kira."

Kira was one of the oldest in the group. When she saw Ashleigh and Mona approach she smiled happily.

"Hi, Kira," Ashleigh said with a big smile. "I'm glad you could make it! This is my friend, Mona. She's another horse nut."

Kira beamed back at them. "Hi, Ashleigh! Nice to meet you, Mona. This is so neat. Wow! All these horses! Who are the ones in the next paddock?"

"The broodmares," Ashleigh answered. "The moms," she clarified when Kira gave her a questioning look. "We have to sell the yearlings, but the broodmares stay here all the time."

"They're so beautiful!" Kira's voice was hushed in

awe, and her eyes were huge as she looked at the mares. "Did some of them used to race?"

"Almost all of them," Ashleigh said. "Some didn't win, but they still have good bloodlines and their babies could be winners. One of them did really well. See that black mare over there?" Ashleigh pointed to Wanderer. "She won a lot of races, and we just sold her yearling at Keeneland for more than we've ever made on a horse. Tonka, the black weanling Kyle likes—the one bossing the others around—is Wanderer's foal this year," Ashleigh explained, motioning to the weanlings' paddock. "My brother named him Tonka after his favorite toy trucks."

At that moment Tonka was definitely asserting himself as boss of the weanlings, staring down anyone who challenged him and leading the other nine yearlings in a merry dash around the paddock.

"He's so awesome, and he looks like he's going to be gorgeous," Kira said.

Ashleigh nodded. "Yeah, I think so, too," she agreed.

"Ash," Mona said, "you haven't shown her Lightning yet."

"The horse you rescued!" exclaimed Kira. "I would love to see her, and you said you had a pony, too."

"Right," Ashleigh stammered, "his name is Moe."

Ashleigh felt like she couldn't breathe. She was

about to say something about Moe really being Rory's, now that she had Lightning. But the words caught in her throat. Again she realized that Kira still knew nothing about the humane society's plans to donate Lightning to Hopewell.

Taking a deep breath, Ashleigh led the whole group to the next pasture to meet Lightning. This would be a sort of test, too, Ashleigh realized. Maybe Kira and the others wouldn't like Lightning. But Ashleigh knew that was unlikely. *What if Lightning and Kira take an immediate liking to each other?*

Today they had put Lightning in a separate dirt paddock beside Moe's pasture, so that she could be ridden. The white mare trotted eagerly to the paddock fence when Ashleigh whistled, but she was wary of the strangers approaching. Mona and Kira were with Ashleigh by the fence. Ashleigh heard Kurt warn the others to stand back.

"Lightning's not really used to a lot of people and she gets nervous," Kurt said.

Moe remained grazing nonchalantly at the far side of his pasture. He knew it wasn't dinner time yet and he wasn't about to be lured away from the fresh grass. With the cooler fall temperatures, sunny days, and nightly frosts, the pastures had greened up again after the hot, dry summer.

Ashleigh fed Lightning a carrot, which she lipped up, but she huffed, eyeing the Hopewell group nervously.

"Can we go inside?" Kira asked. She hadn't taken her eyes off Lightning, who was looking pretty spectacular, Ashleigh had to admit. Her coat gleamed like white satin and her silky mane and tail wafted in the gentle wind. Not a bone was to be seen on her fat and muscular body.

"Sure," Ashleigh said. "But just the three of us. Too many kids in the paddock might frighten Lightning."

Ashleigh opened the gate, and the three of them stepped in. Ashleigh walked over to the mare and clipped a lead to her halter, then led her over to Kira and Mona. Kira had obviously been around horses quite a lot, because she showed no fear as she gently rubbed Lightning's inquisitive nose. "What a pretty girl," she said softly. "How could anyone have treated you so badly? But you look happy now."

Ashleigh took another carrot from her pocket and handed it to Kira. Kira smiled. "Thanks" she said, breaking the carrot in half and offering a piece to Lightning with a natural ease. She looked like she had fed many horses carrots before.

Moe suddenly sensed that he was missing something better than work, and came trotting rapidly across his grassy paddock toward the girls. He let out a loud whinny, just to remind them that he was coming and expected a carrot, too.

They all laughed. "Yes, Moe," Ashleigh called, "I saved some treats for you." Kira ducked under the neighboring fence, where Moe slid to a halt, his nostrils already sniffing out the scent of carrot. Kira fed him the other half of the carrot in her hand.

"You've just made a friend for life," Ashleigh teased. "The fastest way to Moe's heart is through his stomach."

The rest of the Hopewell group were giggling quietly to themselves and eagerly looking on. Lightning had gone back to rooting around the borders of the dirt paddock for stray patches of grass. She seemed to be getting used to having a lot of people around, and didn't seem to mind. Ashleigh heard Sally explain that the white horse was Lightning—the horse Ashleigh had rescued—and they began to bombard Ashleigh with questions.

"When you found her, did she really look as bad as that picture in the newspaper?" Kyle asked.

Ashleigh nodded. "My friend, Mona, was with me." Ashleigh looked at Mona, who flushed. "We found her together. We'd gotten lost . . . then we found her by accident and almost got shot." Ashleigh quickly retold the tale of that adventure-filled day.

"Really? You almost got shot? Wow!"

Ashleigh realized she was playing it up for her audience, but they obviously loved it. She glanced at Mona, who continued the story.

"But Lightning's owner missed, and we galloped out of there. I've never been so scared in my life!" Mona said.

That wasn't an exaggeration, Ashleigh thought. She remembered too well how frightened they both were—scared out of their wits, tired, cold, and completely lost.

"But you went back to feed her, right?" Kyle asked. "I didn't read it in the paper, but someone told me."

"We did go and feed her, but Kurt was the one who actually went up to her owner's place and brought her back here," Ashleigh said.

Kurt was standing with Sally and Ashleigh's parents behind the group of kids pressed against the fence. He gave Ashleigh an embarrassed look, but the kids had already turned around in his direction. Of course they all already knew Kurt from the volunteer work he did at Hopewell.

"You didn't tell us, Kurt," one of them called out accusingly, "that you helped save Lightning!"

Kurt shrugged and looked like he wanted to crawl into the nearest hole to avoid all the eyes focused on him. Ashleigh grinned at him, and he frowned back, but there was a twinkle in his eyes.

Then someone asked, "Can you ride Lightning for us, Ashleigh?"

Ashleigh had already been prepared for that kind of question. Kurt had Lightning's tack ready by the paddock fence, and with his help, Ashleigh tacked her up. Then Kurt gave her a leg up into the saddle.

Lightning was acting fidgety with all the watching eyes. Sally hushed the chattering kids, but Lightning didn't relax until Ashleigh walked her to the far end of the paddock and circled her several times. When Ashleigh asked for a trot, Lightning changed gaits immediately, and Ashleigh began posting, rising in the saddle with the mare's outside shoulder. Ashleigh made a circle at the far end of the paddock, keeping Lightning away from the crowd, and hoping she would settle down.

Ashleigh knew too well that Lightning was not used to crowds, especially young and noisy ones, and could suddenly blow up. Before she'd come to Edgardale, Lightning had led a horribly solitary life.

"It's okay, girl," Ashleigh said as she felt the mare tense up when they headed toward the far end of the paddock where everyone was gathered. "I know they're noisy, but they only want to see how good you are."

Lightning had quieted a little. Still, Ashleigh thought she needed a little more time to adjust. She trotted her in small circles and figure eights in the center of the paddock, until Lightning seemed to be paying close attention to her commands, flicking her ears back and forth attentively. Ashleigh halted her, and then walked back to the gate.

She stopped Lightning a few yards from the fence and prepared to dismount.

Kira called over to her. "Do you think I could I try to ride her, Ashleigh? Just at a walk?" Kira glanced at Sally.

Sally nodded. Kurt brought Kira into the paddock. "I'll lead you," he said, walking with her to Lightning's side.

Ashleigh dismounted and held Lightning's reins. Kurt gave Kira a leg-up into the saddle. She put her feet into the stirrups, and grinned broadly. Ashleigh knew Lightning was used to all the new faces by now, and would be okay with Kira. It was as if she knew she was with friends and was in no danger.

"Okay, I'm ready," Kira called. "It feels really good to sit in a saddle again! Oh, wow!" She waved to her friends in the group. "Watch me, guys!"

Kira reached forward to pat Lightning's neck, then sat back in perfect position. Kurt took over from Ashleigh, and led Lightning and Kira around a large circle at a walk.

"Can I try to walk her on my own?" Kira asked, after Kurt had gone around a few times. "I won't try to do anything else . . . just walk her. I've had lessons."

"I know you have," Ashleigh heard Kurt say. "Okay, why not? She looks like she's behaving herself, and she's not going to run off on you, but I'll stay close, okay?"

"Okay," Kira said, gathering up the reins. She urged Lightning into a walk, making a large circle. Kira was giving gentle, almost unobservable, commands and Lightning was listening. They made a series of figure eights, and then turned down an imaginary center line, stopping gracefully on a dime.

Kira's expression was one of pure concentration, but pure pleasure, too. She looked thrilled. Ashleigh felt so proud of Lightning, who was being very attentive, flicking her ears back and forth and responding promptly to Kira's commands. Ashleigh wondered if horses could sense an illness and would respond with extra sensitivity, just like she'd seen them do around young animals and children. Somehow, although they couldn't see where they placed their massive hooves, they never stepped on their young.

Still, watching Kira ride Lightning, Ashleigh felt a pang of jealousy. She liked Kira a lot, but she absolutely did not want her to have this kind of rapport with Lightning. It was just too hard—and Kira didn't even know that this wasn't just a one-shot lucky ride!

Ashleigh forced her mean and confused feelings aside and walked over to help Kira dismount. When her parents took the rest of the group inside to see the barn, Kira stayed with Ashleigh and Mona as they untacked Lightning. Kira was grinning from ear to ear.

"Wow, you looked great up there, Kira," Mona said, smiling. Then she glanced at Ashleigh.

Ashleigh tried to smile back, but her bottom lip was trembling. She ducked her head under the saddle flap and fumbled with the girth.

"I think I'll put her inside now," Ashleigh said. "It's almost her dinner time anyway."

Mona carried Lightning's saddle and Kira carried the mare's bridle as Ashleigh walked ahead, leading Lightning toward the barn.

"Wow, it's a lot bigger than ours," Kira said as they entered the barn.

"Well, we've got a lot of horses," Ashleigh managed a smile. Everything she said seemed to rub in the notion that she shouldn't keep Lightning. Her family *did* have a lot of horses, after all. Did she really need Lightning?

Once Lightning was in her stall and crunching on her evening feed, the girls leaned over the stall door and talked horses. Kira was so enthusiastic and seemed to be eating up her time at Edgardale. Ashleigh tried to forget her twinges of jealousy and just enjoy being with Mona and her new friend.

When the group was ready to leave, Sally thanked the Griffens profusely. "I can't tell you how great this was for these kids. They've gone through so much, and they need so badly to have some fun, and laugh and joke," Sally said.

Kira went into Lightning's stall to say good-bye.

Sally put a hand on Ashleigh's shoulder and looked her in the eye. "When you're ready, you and your parents should come over and visit me at the center again. We can talk. I've already spoken to your parents, and I know what you must be going through."

The lump had returned to Ashleigh's stomach. She looked back at Sally and tried to smile. "Okay," she said, barely making a sound.

Sally turned to Ashleigh's parents and smiled. "Thanks again—I can't tell you how much this means to us." Ashleigh had the feeling she was talking about more than just their visit. *She means that adopting Lightning would mean a lot to them, doesn't she?*

Kira was the last one into the van. "Bye, Ashleigh. Come see us soon!" she called. Ashleigh waved back.

Then Sally climbed behind the wheel. "Okay, buddies, are we ready to roll?"

The van headed out the Edgardale drive, the voices of the Hopewell kids trailing behind it. "Bye!" "Thank you!" "Bye, Ashleigh!" "Bye, Tonka!"

Ashleigh felt empty inside as she waved them goodbye and stood in the drive, even after the van had disappeared out of sight. It was already growing dark. Finally, she turned to help bring in the horses and give them their evening feeds.

11

"I can see that it's going to be a hard decision for you to make," Mona said as they sat in Lightning's stall. The mare had finished her feed and was now pulling mouthfuls of hay from her hay net. The stall was warm and cozy, although it was freezing outside. The barn doors had been shut tight against the chilly night, and only a few lights were left on. It was very quiet. Everyone else had returned to the house.

"At first I thought you were crazy when you didn't say straight out that you were going to keep Lightning," Mona continued. "But after today, I can understand. It's really a hard decision. And those poor kids—they're all so nice. I really like Kira."

"She's cool, isn't she?" Ashleigh agreed.

"So what are you going to do?"

Ashleigh picked up a blade of hay and chewed it thoughtfully. She frowned. "I think I want to go over and see Hopewell again. Sally wanted me to talk to her, too."

"She seemed real nice, too," Mona said. "You can tell she really wants Lightning to go to Hopewell. But I don't think she would try to talk you into giving her up."

"I don't think she will, either," Ashleigh said "But I *do* want to talk to her."

"You won't really give up Lightning, will you, Ash?" Mona asked.

"I'm not sure," Ashleigh said, truthfully.

Ashleigh had to do a lot of thinking over the next few days. She knew she was stalling, but there were plenty of things to distract her, too. Go Gen, one of the broodmares, came up lame, and Ashleigh's parents were afraid that she might have developed laminitis— a painful and untreatable hoof condition that could lead to an animal having to be put down. Fortunately, when Dr. Frankel examined the mare, he was able to reassure the Griffens.

"It's only an abscess," he said after removing Go Gen's shoe and carefully examining her hoof. "She must have stepped on a splinter or a bit of gravel that's worked its way up into her hoof. I'll drain it and give her some antibiotics. She'll need to have the foot soaked in Epsom salts for forty-five minutes or so, three times a day to draw the infection out. Call me if there's no improvement in the next few days."

When the vet finished treating Go Gen and Kurt led the broodmare off to her stall, Dr. Frankel turned to Ashleigh. "How's the white mare doing?" he asked with a smile.

"Come see," Ashleigh said, leading him outside to the paddock where Lightning and Moe were grazing. Ashleigh whistled, and Lightning eagerly trotted over to the fence. Ashleigh glanced over to the vet.

"Are you sure this is the same horse?" he teased Ashleigh.

She grinned proudly, for the moment forgetting Lightning's uncertain future.

"You deserve a medal for the job you've done, young lady."

"I've been riding her, too," Ashleigh said. "Kurt's been helping me train her, and she's doing great."

Again the vet smiled. "I'm always glad to see a happy ending. Good work! She should make a wonderful pleasure horse for you."

"Yes, she will," Ashleigh replied, but her smile had vanished. *Or for someone else,* she thought.

Ashleigh tried not to let her decision overwhelm

her, but she was falling behind in her homework again. Being with Lightning was more important than homework right now, and her parents didn't scold her for spending more time in the barn than she did studying. The days were short, and she never got back to the house until after dark. When she finally got to her room to study, she couldn't concentrate. End of term tests were fast approaching, and Ashleigh knew she'd be unprepared.

"Ash," Caroline said one night. "Why don't you just tell them you're going to keep Lightning? That's what you want, and you've been a pain to live with ever since those kids from Hopewell were here—not that you haven't always been a pain. But I for one am tired of your moping."

For a change, Ashleigh felt no need to snap back at her sister's criticism. She shrugged. "I just don't know what to do, Caro."

"Well, that's a first." Caro sounded surprised. "When have you ever *not* known what to do? When it comes to you and horses, the horse always wins."

"Not this time," Ashleigh said. But this time it seemed that Lightning would win either way. It was only Ashleigh who could lose.

*   *   *

The next afternoon Kurt met Ashleigh as she was heading to the barn. "I'm going over to help at Hopewell for an hour or so. Would you like to come with me?"

Ashleigh hesitated, then nodded. She knew it was something she had to do.

A half hour later, Kurt parked his truck in Hopewell's drive, and he and Ashleigh got out. The playground was deserted, but they heard lively voices coming from the direction of the barn. "Let's see what's going on," Kurt said.

The barn felt warm and welcoming after the chill outside, but as soon as they stepped inside, Mortimer the duck, self-appointed guard-bird, let out several ear-piercing quacks and quickly waddled toward them. Sally stuck her head around one of the stall partitions.

"Well, look who's here. This is a surprise, Ashleigh, but I'm so glad to see you," Sally said. "Hi, Kurt. You've got some eager kids waiting to show you what they've been doing this afternoon." She shooed the duck gently away. "All right, enough, Mortimer," she called. "These are friends."

The duck gave a final quack but stood his ground, eyeing the new arrivals.

Ashleigh heard giggles, and several smiling faces

peeked out of another stall. "We're not ready yet, Kurt," Kyle called. "You can't look."

"Promise I won't until you tell me it's okay," Kurt answered.

Kira came into the barn while they were waiting, and her face lit up when she saw Ashleigh. "I didn't know you'd be here today," she said.

Ashleigh smiled at her new friend. "Kurt was coming over and asked if I wanted to come along," she explained.

There was another burst of mischievous giggles from the stall, and Kira looked over curiously. "What's going on?"

"They have a surprise for us. We're waiting for them to get ready," Kurt explained.

"Okay, now we're ready," one of the children called. "Close your eyes."

Ashleigh went along with the game and closed her eyes with everyone else.

"Okay, you can open them now," one of the boys cried.

Standing in the barn aisle, surrounded by six of the center's younger patients, was Barney, the black-and-white goat, completely decked out in ribbons and bows. Some circled his neck; others hung from his horns. Each of his legs had been wrapped like a vividly colored May pole. In fact, hardly any of his coat was visible through the splendid adornments.

The poor goat was a sight. Ashleigh and the others burst out laughing. "Oh, my, what a work of art!" Sally exclaimed. "The most beautiful goat I've ever laid eyes on."

"Definitely," Kurt agreed, then added to the patient animal, "Looking good, Barney."

The children giggled.

"But I wonder what Barney thinks of all of this?" Sally asked.

They had their answer when Barney immediately ducked his head, took a mouthful of the ribbons wrapped around his foreleg and began to chew. He seemed to be enjoying the meal, too. That got everyone laughing again.

"I think I'll go supervise the unwrapping procedure," Kurt said with a smile and headed into Barney's stall.

"I'll help," Kira offered, following Kurt.

"So," Sally said pleasantly to Ashleigh. "Would you like to look around some more?"

"If you don't mind, but I don't want to interrupt anything," Ashleigh said.

"You're not," Sally assured her. "Let's do the grand tour. Ask me all the questions you'd like." Sally led the way through the barn, pointing out the big box stall that would house any horse the center acquired, and the immaculate storage rooms. They passed the stall the chickens, Daisy and Pumpkin, called home and saw Olie, the potbellied pig, curled up on his straw bed next door, sound asleep. Two of the several barn cats followed them.

Ashleigh could find no fault with the facilities. Lightning would be comfortable and in good company. Hopewell seemed so cozy and full of good cheer. Ashleigh didn't see anything to make her doubt that it would make a great home for Lightning.

"You said you know a lot about horses," Ashleigh said to Sally.

"Oh, yes, and I love them," Sally replied. "I grew up on a training farm, so my background's kind of like yours, only my family never owned any of the horses, they only took them in for training."

"What kind of training?"

"Racing. I used to help my folks out by exercise riding the horses." Sally chuckled. "Of course, that wasn't exactly a sacrifice. I loved doing it."

Sally had Ashleigh's full attention. "You used to exercise ride? That's my dream! I want to be a jockey."

"So did I," Sally said, "but, as you can see, I grew too much. I was already five foot five when I was your age and still growing. The kids in school used to call me the jolly thin giant."

"That was mean," Ashleigh said.

"Yeah. It hurt my feelings a lot at the time, especially because I wanted so badly to be a jockey. But now I can look back and laugh. I don't mind being tall and thin so much anymore. Anyway, I had to change my goals and went into hunter jumpers instead."

"My friend, Mona, wants to own a jumping stable some day."

"And you, no doubt, want to own a Thoroughbred breeding farm," Sally said.

"How did you know?" Ashleigh exclaimed.

"Just a calculated guess," Sally said. "And you're getting all the training you need on your parents' farm."

Once again Ashleigh was reminded of how lucky she was to live on a breeding farm. Sally interrupted her thoughts.

"I hope you realize, Ashleigh, that I don't want to pressure you in any way. I'm sad that a decision like the one you have to make rests on such young shoulders."

"My parents said that, too."

"I'm not surprised. But everyone has faith that you can handle the decision. I just want you to know that if Lightning does come to live here, she'll get the very best care and tons and tons of love. I'd bring her back to you myself if I thought things were going otherwise. You also have my promise that you could come visit her and ride her as often as you wanted," Sally assured her.

"Really?" Ashleigh asked, feeling suddenly better. That wouldn't be so bad. Ashleigh thought about the sparkle in Kira's eyes when she rode Lightning and how thrilled the other kids had been when they'd toured Edgardale.

"Kurt told me," Sally went on, "about how the humane society patrons acted when they came to Edgardale. They were completely off-base, but I don't think they understood the situation. They're only involved with raising money for a worthy cause and the prestige that goes along with it. They depend on people like you and me to look after and love the animals who are adopted."

"They'll still be trying to take all the credit if Lightning came here," Ashleigh said sagely. "It will look better for them, won't it?"

Sally responded, her voice firm. "You and Mona and Kurt saved that mare, and I'll make sure everyone knows it."

"Thanks," Ashleigh said. She felt a lot better. But she felt strange, too, as if a decision had already been made, although Ashleigh hadn't decided anything either way. Still, her mind felt more clear.

Kurt called to them from the other end of the barn aisle and walked toward them. "Hate to say it, Ashleigh, but we've got to head back," he said.

"Oh, Ashleigh, do you have to go so soon?" Kira asked. "We didn't even get a chance to talk."

"I'm sorry, Kira. But I'll see you again soon," Ashleigh said. "We have to get back to bring in the horses. Why don't you give me a call, or I'll call you?" Ashleigh glanced over to Sally. "Is Kira allowed to make phone calls?"

Sally laughed. "Of course she is, as long as she doesn't hog the phone so that other kids can't use it. We have a set limit. Fifteen minutes max per phone call unless it's an emergency."

"Can I call you tonight?" Kira asked eagerly. "I want to hear all about Lightning. It was so great being able to ride her—just to know that I can still ride and haven't forgotten everything."

"Okay, call me," Ashleigh said as the two girls exchanged a parting wave.

Ashleigh was silent through much of the drive back to Edgardale. Finally Kurt broke into her thoughts. "It isn't easy, is it?" he said quietly.

"I was thinking about Kira. And Lightning," Ashleigh added.

"Well, you're a brave young lady, Ashleigh," Kurt said. "No matter what you do, I'm behind you, one hundred percent." Still, Ashleigh's heart was heavy with the weight of her decision.

When they arrived back at Edgardale, both of them went straight to their evening routine of bringing in the horses and feeding them. Now that the weather was so cool, none of the mares went back out into the paddock for the night. Instead, they were buckled into blankets and spent the night in their warm stalls. It was the summer routine in reverse. In the summer, because of the heat, the horses were sometimes kept in their stalls during the day, and only put out to pasture during the cooler nights.

When the evening chores were finished and everyone was heading into the house, Ashleigh asked her parents if she could stay out in the barn. "I'm not hungry," she said. "I don't want any dinner. I just need to be with Lightning for a while."

At first her parents frowned. Ashleigh expected them to say that skipping meals wasn't healthy, but then she saw their expressions soften a little. They knew she'd been at Hopewell that afternoon, and sensed that she was down to the wire and had a decision to make.

"Okay, you can stay out here a while," her mother said, gently. "But not so long that you don't have time for your homework. I'll put a plate aside for you to warm up if you get hungry."

Her parents left. The barn was quiet except for the horse sounds—the quiet sounds of hay being pulled from nets, a soft whicker here and there, a hoof stomped, a contented sigh. Ashleigh sat down in Lightning's stall and looked at the mare who was contentedly eating her hay.

"Lightning," Ashleigh called to her, "I want to keep you so much."

Lightning nickered at the sound of Ashleigh's voice.

"I've dreamed about you being mine for so long, and now. . . ."

Lightning stepped away from her hay net, lowered her head, and huffed softly into Ashleigh's hair.

"I just don't know what to do," Ashleigh said, starting to cry. "I pretended you were mine from the day Mona and I found you. But Kira and those kids at Hopewell need you, too. Maybe even more than I do. Oh, I wish you could stay!"

Lightning continued whuffing soft breaths into

Ashleigh's dark hair. She may not have understood Ashleigh's words, but she seemed to understand the emotion behind them.

"I wish you could talk to me and tell me what you think," Ashleigh sobbed. "I want you to stay here with me more than anything. But those kids at Hopewell will love you, too. You liked Kira, didn't you, girl? You might even help them all get better if you lived there. My mom says I should never act selfish. Is it selfish to want to keep you?"

Ashleigh got up to get some grooming brushes. Lightning's coat was already shining and clean, but brushing her helped Ashleigh think, and Lightning certainly loved it. Her muscles rippled. For the mare, it was just an unexpected massage. For Ashleigh it was time for decisions.

Ashleigh hugged Lightning, put away the brushes, and went up to the house. She knew what she was going to do. It was as if she had known all day, but hadn't been able to admit it to herself until then. She would talk to her parents and ask them to help with her plan.

12

The Saturday before Christmas, the Griffens invited the Hopewell children to a party in the barn at Edgardale. The whole family had helped to decorate the barn with fresh wreaths and red bows. The air was filled with the scent of pine and there was a stocking on each of the horses' stalls.

Ashleigh helped pile plates high with holiday cookies and stood a big bowl of fruit punch on a table at one end of the barn. They put out baskets of apples and carrots to feed to the horses. Caroline brought out her tape deck and a tape of Christmas songs. Mr. Griffen had strung colored lights around each stall partition, and Kurt brought a brightly wrapped gift for each of the children. Even the weather was Christmasy—there had been a light dusting of snow the night before and everything outside was coated in a fine white powder, their first snow that winter.

Normally Ashleigh would have been thrilled, and she tried to get into the spirit, too, but she was filled with mixed emotions.

Ashleigh had spent all morning in Lightning's stall, grooming the mare from head to toe. First she brushed her and rubbed her coat with a soft cloth. Then she carefully combed Lightning's long mane and tail, and cleaned and polished her hoofs. She took the new leather halter from the hook outside the stall and slipped it over Lightning's head. The tack store had attached the brass plate inscribed with Lightning's name to the cheek strap, and it looked just right. Lastly, Ashleigh wrapped a wide red velvet ribbon she'd bought in town around Lightning's neck, and carefully tied it in a huge bow.

She stood back to look at her work and nodded in satisfaction. Lightning couldn't have looked more beautiful. The best present anyone could ever hope to receive. Tears welled up in her eyes, but Ashleigh fought them back.

A moment later she heard the sound of happy voices, as the kids from Hopewell arrived. They streamed into the barn, with ohs and ahs of excitement when they saw the decorations, the plates of food, and the pile of presents on the table.

"Are those for us?" Kyle asked.

"They sure are," Kurt answered, "but not until after the pony ride."

"Pony ride?"

"We've saddled up our pony, Moe," Mr. Griffen said. "And Mona brought over her pony, Silver, too. Who wants to go first?"

There was a chorus of cries. "I do! I do!"

Sally settled the matter. "We'll go in alphabetical order. Andrew and Corinne, you're first."

"Follow me," Kurt said, leading them out the side door of the barn where Rory and Mona were holding the ponies.

The others stayed inside, nibbling on cookies and feeding and patting the horses until it was their turn to ride. Kira wandered from stall to stall, talking to the horses and helping the younger children feed them treats.

Ashleigh looked at all the happy faces and tried to smile back and answer all their questions. All of the horses had been kept inside for the party and they were looking over their stall doors inquisitively.

"I like the one with the big, white blaze."

"That's Jolita," Ashleigh said.

"And what about that black one?"

"That's Wanderer, our best mare. One of her daughters is winning some big races this year."

The questions went on until the last two children returned to the barn, rosy-cheeked from their rides. "That was so much fun! I've never ridden a pony before, but it wasn't scary at all!" a little girl named Wendy cried.

Kyle nodded his head vigorously. "I wish I could ride every day. It would be so neat if we had a horse at Hopewell."

"Okay, everyone," Mrs. Griffen called. "Time for presents. Kurt, do you want to play Santa?"

Kurt stepped over to the table. "*Ho, ho, ho,*" he said, deepening his voice. "Do I look like Santa Claus?"

There was a chorus of giggles. "No. You're not fat enough, and you don't have a beard."

"I guess I'll have to be his helper then." He picked up a package. "What have we here? It says 'Jonathan.'"

For the next several minutes the barn was filled with the sound of ripping paper and happy shouts. When the last present was opened and the discarded paper cleared from the barn floor, Ashleigh spoke up. "Wait. There's one more present."

The kids looked at her in surprise.

"It's for all of you." Ashleigh walked to Lightning's stall, opened the half door and clipped a lead to her halter. Then she led her out into the barn. "Here she is. Lightning's my present to all of you. Merry Christmas."

She heard gasps of surprise. "Really? Do you mean it?"

Ashleigh led Lightning further down the barn aisle, until she was standing in front of Kira, and handed over Lightning's lead rope. "I know you'll love her as much as I do and you'll take good care of her," Ashleigh said, her voice trembling. "And she'll make all of you as happy as she's made me." She had to blink back her tears. "But I hope you don't mind if I'm around a lot to see her."

"Are you serious?" Kira asked, incredulous, but her face was lit with joy.

Ashleigh nodded, too choked up to say anything.

Kira threw her arms around Ashleigh. "Thank you, Ashleigh. Thank you so much! She's the most amazing present any of us could ever have!" Then she looked at Lightning, who was shaking her head, and trying to nibble at the bow around her neck. Kira stroked her nose and combed her fingers through her thick white forelock. Lightning didn't seem fazed by all the commotion; in fact she seemed to be enjoying center-stage.

Sally and Ashleigh's parents were chatting happily with an older man who'd just come in through the barn door. *He must be the man from the local paper,*

Ashleigh thought. Sally had been true to her word. When Ashleigh had told Sally what she'd planned to do, Sally had promised that the story would be reported properly. She'd called a reporter friend and invited him to the party.

From the look on everyone's faces, Ashleigh knew in her heart that she'd done the right thing.

"Just take good care of her," she said, blinking back tears. "She's really, really special."

"We will!" the Hopewell kids chorused happily.

Sally walked over and put an arm around Ashleigh's shoulders. "I know how hard this is for you, but you're doing a wonderful thing. I can't thank you enough. Lightning is going to help a lot of children. And we're going to love her and take very special care of her, right, guys?" she called to the kids.

"Right!"

"And remember, you can visit any time," Sally added.

Ashleigh smiled bravely and laid her cheek against Lightning's neck. "You be good, and don't forget, I'll always love you."

Lightning whickered softly and touched her nose to Ashleigh's shoulder as if to say she understood.

JOANNA CAMPBELL was born and raised in Norwalk, Connecticut and grew up loving horses. She eventually owned a horse of her own and took lessons, specializing in open jumping. She still rides when possible and started her two young granddaughters on lessons. In addition to publishing many books for young readers, she is the author of four adult novels. She has also sung and played the piano professionally and owned an antique business. She now lives on the coast of Maine with her husband, Ian Bruce. She has two children, Kimberly and Kenneth, and three grand-children.

THOROUGHBRED

If you enjoyed this book, then you'll love reading all the books in the THOROUGHBRED series!

THOROUGHBRED

◆◆◆◆◆◆◆◆◆◆◆◆◆◆◆◆◆◆◆◆◆◆◆◆◆◆◆◆◆◆◆◆◆◆

All books are
$4.50 U.S./$5.50 Canadian

◆◆◆◆◆◆◆◆◆◆◆◆◆◆◆◆◆◆◆◆◆◆◆◆◆◆◆◆◆◆◆◆◆◆